Captured Mafia Princess

A Dark Kidnap Romance

Em Brown

Contents

Chapter One

Kai

"It's by invitation only," I tell Andrian Plotnikov, who unleashes a string of Russian oaths, all of which I'm familiar with because Andrian curses as often as the sun shines out here in California and because I learned my fair share of Russian growing up in the conurbation of Heihe and Blagoveshchensk.

Sitting at my desk, I watch as my dog, Athena, plays with the stray cat I picked up the other night. I'm amazed at how the two seem to have hit it off almost instantly, not unlike Andrian and I when we first met on the streets of Blagoveshchensk as teens.

"*Yebat'yego v rot! Yebat'yego v rot!*" Andrian repeats. "When is this auction?"

"Could be as early as ten days," I reply. "Callaghan knows he has to unload the asset fast before we get to him."

Ten days is not a long time but doable for us to retrieve the laptop containing coding for HITDS, High Impact Tactical Droid System, highly classified artificial intelligence from SVATR, a Silicon Valley tech company that has contracts with the Department of Defense to develop the latest state-of-the-art military equipment.

It was smart of Liam Callaghan, a small time Irish mafia boss, to auction off SVATR's system to a limited number of people, even if it meant he might not get as much money in the end because, like Andrian said, we're gunning for him. I was the one who had orchestrated the heist. HITDS is mine to sell, not Callaghan's.

"We should be certain about the auction date," Andrian says. "If my contact in Syria hears anything, I will let you know. I leave Moscow in a few days, hope sooner. Then we beat shit out of this Liam Callaghan."

"We get the laptop back first," I remind him.

"*Da, da.* You said you wanted to consider all options. Did you decide? Are we going to kidnap the asshole's daughter?"

I hesitate. Last night I had thought to scrap my plan to use Casey to force Callaghan to give up the laptop. But that was before I learned this morning that Callaghan might auction the laptop in only a week and a half.

"Why not kidnap whole family?" Andrian asks.

"The son is in Ireland. Too risky in unfamiliar territory," I answer. "We could take the wife, though I'm not sure how much Callaghan cares about her. My intel shows he's had a number of women on the side."

"Too bad. I would love to see his face when we kill his family in front of him. So, we take only the daughter?"

I don't answer right away. Something about it doesn't sit right with me, though the daughter is the logical best choice. From what I've heard, Liam wants to merge the Callaghans with another mafia family, the Bradys, through marriage. The heir to the latter is a young man named Kenton, who graduated from

Notre Dame two years ahead of Casey. Only, Casey isn't too interested in Kenton.

Because she's interested in me.

I can see it in her eyes. Same way I see it in other women's eyes. Even the most artful women can't hide it.

"The daughter should be relatively easy to kidnap," I say. *Almost too easy.*

"*Khorosho.* Text me when it's done."

"I will."

"But wait until I get back to US before contacting Callaghan. I want to see his face when we threaten to kill his offspring."

"I'll wait to initiate negotiations."

"*Spasibo.* I have news also. I think our leak, it might be Evgeni."

I shake my head. "Too bad. I liked Evgeni."

"Yeah, but he talks too much, you know? Especially with the whores. He was in Boston visiting his brother and went to a brothel run by Callaghan's cousin."

"What are you going to do about it?"

"If I had patience, I would try the Chinese *lingchi*," Andrian says, referring to the death by a thousand cuts dating back to before the Song dynasty. "I like what your triad did last year to a traitor."

A close-knit organization built mostly on blood ties, the *Jing San Triad* does not take lightly to betrayers, one of whom "disappeared" last year, though photos of his dismembered body parts continue to show up.

"I would like to have such a warning," Andrian muses aloud, "to anyone who thinks of fucking me."

"Was it only Evgeni?" I ask. "You had a lot of other hackers on this job."

"I think only Evgeni, but I'm not sure."

I've gone through the handful of my people who were on this joint effort between me and Andrian. On my side, the one most likely to have betrayed me was Michael, and I doubt he did. He died when Callaghan's men ambushed our guys and made off with a laptop that would have fetched me and Andrian eight figures easy.

"Might be worth keeping him alive to see if you can get more info out of him," I suggest, even though there's a good chance Andrian has already shot the guy dead.

"I am giving him opportunity to speak before we cut his balls out," Andrian replies.

"Get as much out of him as you can. We can't afford more fuckups."

"*Da, da.* We get laptop back, no more worries."

After I end my call with Andrian, Athena trots over to me. The stray cat I toyed with naming Maeve leaps onto my desk. She didn't take long to warm up to her new surroundings. I thought she'd be hiding beneath a sofa for several days. She's either fearless or lacks a healthy dose of mistrust.

Kind of like Casey Callaghan.

I pick up my cellphone. Casey had asked to see me again. I had texted her no. She had replied that she would be at Club de Sade tonight if I changed my mind.

Guess I'll be going to the Club de Sade.

Chapter Two

Casey

After reading his text to me last night, I spend almost the entire next morning in my bed thinking about Jack. I don't know much about him other than his first name, that he's a businessman of some kind, and that he likes cats. I'd like to have more information, though I already know the most important thing about him: he's the Dom of my dreams.

Part of me is still stunned by his rejection. I could have sworn he had a good time with me at The Lotus, an uber luxury BDSM club, compared to my regular haunt, Club de Sade. And I thought we connected not just on the BDSM level. I remember how, on our "non-date," he had put his arm around me to keep me warm while we stood in the alley, in the middle of the night, waiting for the stray cat. Maybe the connection was just on my end.

Was there anything I could have done differently to make him want to see me again? I thought he was intrigued by the idea of playing out our kidnapping fantasy? How delicious would that be?

Closing my eyes, I imagine it's the middle of the night. I'm asleep. Suddenly, a hand covers my mouth and nose. It's him.

"Make a sound or move and you'll regret it," he warns me.

I might pretend to struggle.

He slams my head back down on my pillow. "I told you not to move, so now you're going to get punished."

I wonder how he'll punish me? Whatever he does, I'm sure I'll like it. I hope he does something involving rope bondage. I liked the one-legged stand he had tied me in yesterday, though the asymmetry had started to bug me after a while. It's not every day that you come across someone skilled in shibari, and I desperately want to experience what else he can do.

Hopping out of bed, I get dressed, deciding I'll go to the gym and grab a smoothie afterward. I'd drive myself up to Tahoe to hit the slopes, but I really want to see Jack again. Just thinking about him puts knots in my groin.

"Kenton said to me that you don't have to play hard to get with him," my cousin, Hannah, says when she joins me at the gym.

"I'm not," I reply as we head to the elliptical machines.

"So you did go clubbing with this guy Jake?"

"Jack."

We get onto the machines and select a program.

"I don't understand what you could see in this guy that would make you choose him over Kenton," says Hannah.

I raise my brows. "Is my dad paying you to say that?"

"No! But, honestly, what's wrong with Kenton? I mean, I'd date him in a heartbeat."

I perk up. "You should!"

"He's interested in *you.*"

"He's not really. Our dads think we'd make a good match, that's all."

My hand wanders between my legs as I consider t different ways he can punish me. My pussy lips a still sore from the weighted crotch rope he did on m but my clit is alive and ready for arousal. I could g for another round of hard fucking. Even though i had been painful at times last night, I'd do it again just to feel his cock pulsing inside me. As I relive the rough sex we had, I finger myself more intensely until I eventually come.

In some ways, my climax is unsatisfying because it's nothing like what I experienced with Jack. Masturbating is nice, but nothing blows my mind like BDSM. While I can try to do some things solo, it's not nearly as fun. Why dance by yourself if you can dance with a partner? The only thing I don't mind doing solo is snowboarding.

With a sigh, I reach for my phone to check for a text or call from Jack. Still nothing, though I had already checked a few times after waking up. I had texted Jack asking what he decided to do with the stray cat, but I haven't received a response. Is he ghosting me?

"Aaargh," I groan. "I'm obsessing like a high school girl over her crush."

"Kenton is drop dead gorgeous, rich, funny, and he's probably good in bed."

"You have no idea whether he's good in bed or not."

"But he's got that swagger, you know? He's all confident like."

I want to tell her I've been with enough guys to know that a guy's "swagger" usually correlates with *less* ability rather than more, but Hannah doesn't know about my secret passion for BDSM and all the sex partners I've had at Club de Sade.

"He's a player," I say instead.

"That makes him hotter! I mean, it shows you that all these women want him."

"I just don't feel it with Kenton. We don't have anything in common."

"So what do you have in common with this guy Jack?"

To be honest, the only shared interest I know we have is BDSM.

"Chemistry," I reply.

"So you seeing him again tonight? Because some of us were thinking to go clubbing."

I think for a moment. Maybe I shouldn't be so fixed on Jack. He's clearly not as interested in me as I am in him. But what if he does change his mind? I already texted him I'd be at Club de Sade tonight. I'd kick myself if he showed up and I wasn't there. But maybe he senses my interest in him and is panicked by it. It's hard for me to imagine Jack panicked by anything, but a lot of men seem to fear a relationship more than they fear death or public speaking.

However, I was explicit, or I thought I was, that I wasn't looking for a relationship. I just want the sex. He's got to be okay with that.

"So, clubbing tonight with us?" Hannah prompts.

I answer, "I'll think about it."

*****

It's past eight at night, and I still haven't received a text from Jack about the cat. Maybe he didn't see my text. I could try him again, but I don't want to pester him. I'll just go to Club de Sade and hope that he shows up. If he doesn't, I'm going to head to Tahoe and pound my sexual frustrations out on the slopes.

I find my bodyguard, Chase, hanging out in the pool room of our house in Pacific Heights. "Be ready in an hour. Going to the club tonight."

"Your father asked me where you went last night," Chase tells me.

"You told him I was hanging out with my friend Aleisha, right?"

"Yeah, yeah, but he started asking me what I know about her."

"What'd you say?"

"I said I didn't know much about her. What are you going to tell your dad about tonight?"

I run through possible excuses. "How 'bout we say we were with your 'cousin,' Mason? I heard he was feeling down and needed cheering up. We stayed in and binged on musicals."

Mason is Chase's live-in boyfriend, but if my father knew that Chase was gay, he'd fire him.

"You don't like musicals," Chase points out. "You only listen to alternative and punk rock."

"My dad doesn't know that."

Between running his crime ring and sleeping around on my mother, my father doesn't take the time to get to know me much, yet he expects me to do what he wants like I'm one of his loyal goons.

After squaring away my alibi with Chase, I go to my room to pick out my outfit. I want something sexy but not too desperate looking. I don't want to look like Carmen, another Club de Sade member who would love to steal my Dom from me.

"That's right, he's mine," I tell an imaginary Carmen as I pull on a pair of ripped jeans with large cutouts showing my thighs.

I put on a short leather jacket over my cropped tee. Showing off my midriff doesn't go with the winter weather, though it actually hit sixty degrees today in San Francisco. To complete my outfit, I don platform leather motorcycle boots with high heels. I keep my hair simple, tying it back in a ponytail, and add hoop earrings.

Satisfied with my look, I meet up with Chase and hop in my car. While he drives, I look at my phone to see no call or text from Jack still. Should I have reminded him that I'll be at the Club de Sade? I start texting but then I remember that he still hasn't answered my question about the cat, so I text:

Did you get my text about the cat?

I get a text, but it's not from Jack. It's Kenton asking me about going out tonight. Again. I had already told him I was planning on staying in. I text him back that I'm helping Chase with something but that he and our friends should go out without me.

Not wanting to deal with Kenton—he already showed up unannounced at my house yesterday to ask me why I was blowing him off—I put down my phone. It dings.

I growl. It's probably Kenton texting me that I'm a bitch. Because I'm not swooning over him like a "good Irish girl" should. Because I believe that my dad's idea to cement relations with his dad by marrying me off to Kenton is bullshit. The mob needs to come into current century.

My cellphone dings again. I glance at it with no intention of picking it up when I see that the text isn't from Kenton. It's from Jack.

Cat's with me.

My pulse quickens. He's not ghosting me. That's a good sign. I lick my bottom lip as I consider how to respond. I type:

Cool. Going to Club de Sade.

Short and simple. That way he can't read too much into it. I wait anxiously to see if he responds.

He doesn't.

I can't tell if he's read my text or not. There's something quirky about the way his phone is set up. A random set of digits shows up instead of a phone number, so I can't call him. Should I text him asking if he'll be there? Or should I pretend like I don't care?

A text comes in:

Have fun.

My shoulders sag. I purse my lips and make a raspberry sound.

"What's the matter?" Chase inquires.

"Doesn't seem like Jack will be at the club tonight," I reply, putting down my phone in disappointment.

"Sorry about that. He was fucking hot. But you always find someone to play with."

Yeah, but I have little interest in playing with anyone if they aren't Jack. I don't even feel like going to the club now. Leaning my head back, I toy with the idea of telling Chase to turn the car around. But if I misread Jack and he's done with me, I need to move on. Best way to move on is hooking up with someone else at the club.

So I let Chase drive to the area south of Market that used to be an industrial district before it was gentrified. The Club de Sade is in one of the warehouses that wasn't converted into condos.

Recognizing me and Chase, the bouncer lets us in. I decide I'll look for Aleisha first to vent my sorrows to before I consider playing with anyone. But as I step into the area where members can sit at tables to watch the action, my breath stops.

It's *him*.

Chapter Three

Kai

From the corners of my eyes, I see Casey and her bodyguard have entered the club, but I continue to face one of the stalls near the corner of the club where a dominatrix is engaging in CBT with her sub. He lies naked on a coffee table with a cage around his balls and penis while his Mistress hovers over him with a violet wand.

I see Chase go and sit at a table in the far corner. Casey approaches me.

"Your text made it sound like you weren't going to be here," she says.

"In that case: surprise," I respond.

She smiles. "I like surprises, especially this one. Mind if I sit down?"

I pull a chair out for her.

Sitting down, she glances at the mug before me. "Tea?"

I nod.

"I think I'll have tea too," she says, then waves at a server. After requesting a cup of tea, she turns back to me. "I'm glad you changed your mind."

"You sure you don't want to change *your* mind?" I return.

She leans in toward me. "I'm not afraid of you."

I stare back at her. *You should be, princess.*

"Why not?"

"Because I trust you."

Mentally, I shake my head. Stupid, stupid girl.

"You're very trusting, then," I say.

"I don't know. I just have a good feeling about you."

She looks at me with those sparkling blue eyes of hers. I almost want to ask if she'd still have that feeling if she knew I made a guy who tried to double-cross me blow his own brains out?

"So I assume you're gonna play tonight," she says.

"Why would you assume that?" I return.

"Why else would you be here?"

"This club is about voyeurism."

She feigns a pout. "Why watch? It's not nearly as fun as being the action."

"Does princess have a problem sitting still?"

"Sure, after I've been spanked nice and good."

"Ever been spanked so hard you couldn't sit?"

"No," she replies but continues to smile. "You have experience with that?"

I had a sub who was seriously into pain. She'd stick needles into her own tits. And I once caned her ass hard enough she bled.

I stare into Casey's eyes. "Yes."

She seems taken aback. "Really?"

"You're still in the minor leagues of BDSM, princess."

At first she looks down and frowns, but then she lifts her chin. "I'm meant for the big leagues."

"Takes time, princess."

"I'm a quick learner."

"Yeah? You get good grades in school?"

"No," she admits, "but that's because the subjects were boring. BDSM is anything but."

I shake my head. She's like a dog on a bone. If I wasn't interested in kidnapping her and using her as ransom, her persistence might annoy me, but right now, it kind of amuses me.

"What's in there?" she asks, noticing a duffel bag on the floor near my chair.

"You'll find out."

Her face lights up. I can kind of see how her dad might like spoiling her.

"Good," she declares. "What are we waiting for, then?"

"You haven't gotten your tea yet."

"I'll drink it later. I'm not actually that thirsty—not for tea anyway."

Corny but cute. I survey the available booths and select one that has a small side table and a wooden dining chair with a vertical back. It's in the middle of the line of booths and visible to the most amount of people. About a dozen patrons sit in the audience area, some engaged in conversation, others watching the activities in the stalls.

"Everything comes off," I tell Casey when we reach our stall.

Without hesitation, she takes off her coat while I unpack my bag on the table, taking out cords of rope and an anal hook. She undoes her shoes, then whips off her jeans. I hear a whistle from the crowd and wonder if she's one of those people who likes to show off her body, snapping booty shots and posting them on a social media app for the world to see. Her shirt comes off next, leaving her only in her bra and panties.

Crossing my arms in front of me, I watch as she removes her underwear. My gaze takes in her body from head to toe, noting her tattoo of handcuffs at the top of an ass cheek and, when she turns around to face me, her trimmed patch of pubic hair.

She gives me a perky smile, confident that I like what I see. I do. But then, I haven't come across a naked woman I couldn't appreciate. However, I'm less inclined to stick figures and like that Casey has some muscle. Her tits are nice too and proportional to her body.

"Turn around and show your audience the goods," I say after she removes her bra.

She does, and I have a view of her ass. Warmth stirs in me as I recall how I paddled her backside red the first time we played. I'm going to go for a more lasting bruise next time.

Tonight, I decide to start her off in a relatively easy position and direct her to sit backwards in the chair. Grabbing cords of rope, I bind her right wrist and knee together to one stile of the chair. I do the same to her left wrist and knee with the other stile, then I tie her ankles to the bottom of the front legs. Half her ass hangs off the seat, giving me a nice view of her asshole. Next I fit a head harness with the red ball gag onto her. I should give her a physical cue for a safe word, but she won't need it just yet. However, she doesn't know that. I let the audience admire the view of her tethered to the chair before grabbing a flogger. Taking my time, I warm up her back and ass.

Squatting down behind her, I run my hands over her back, her hips, her thighs before groping her buttocks. I knead the spheres before giving them a good hard smack. Reaching for her chest, I fondle her breasts, tenderly groping them before harshly mauling. I pinch and pull at her nipples, making her grunt. Standing up, I walk to the other side of the chair. Her gaze follows my every move. I reach my hand between the vertical slats of the chair back and pull her nipple, twisting it till she yelps against the ball gag. I torture the pink nub until she pants. Her squeals are high and loud against the ball gag. From my pocket I pull out a set of nipple clamps connected by a short chain. After attaching them, I tug on the chain. She whimpers.

"Like that?" I ask.

She probably doesn't, but she knows there's only one answer.

"Yes, Sir," comes her muffled answer.

"Want me to pull harder?"

Her eyes widen a little. Again, there's only one answer.

After a brief hesitation, she answers, "Yes, Sir."

"That doesn't sound like a very enthusiastic yes," I admonish.

She responds with a louder, more emphatic, "Yes, Sir!"

I pull on the chain. The clamps snap off. She cries out.

"My bad," I say. "Let's try that again."

I affix the clamps back on and pull the chain as far as I can. She starts to squirm in the chair. I yank the clamps off again, making her cry out again.

"Want to try a third time?" I ask.

I know I'm being an asshole, but she wanted this.

When she doesn't answer right away, I slap the side of her face.

"Yes, Sir," she mumbles into her gag.

I put the nipple clamps back on and pull on the chain. She grips the chair, bracing herself. Instead of pulling on the chain again, I drop it. Her body relaxes in relief.

Reaching into my other pocket, I pull out several small weights with hooks. "We're going to play a little game. For every time you come, you get one of these."

Demonstrating, I hang one of the weights on the chain connecting her nipple clamps. She grunts.

"That one's free," I say as I put the weights back in my pocket.

Standing up, I walk around to squat behind her. I've got a nice view of her ass and her pussy lips touching the chair.

I reach between her thighs. "You're soaking wet, like the slut that you are. We're gonna have to disinfect the whole chair when we're done."

Wanting to see her ass quiver, I smack both cheeks with my palms, then part her flesh to see more of her asshole. I graze my finger over it. "We'll see some action here today."

I fondle her between the legs, just enough to get her moaning, then slide two digits into her snatch and stroke her. It doesn't take long before her cunt is flexing on my fingers. She lifts her ass to improve the angle of my penetration. I finger fuck her in earnest.

When I feel her close, I say, "Come if you're a slut."

Her body stiffens, then trembles against the chair.

"That's one," I say, placing one of the weights from my pocket onto a table beside her.

I continue to shove my fingers into her. Fresh off her first orgasm, she's quick to come a second time.

"That's two."

I place another weight on the table. She groans. Her pussy is still flexing. I pull my fingers out and bring her to a third orgasm by fondling her clit.

I place another weight on the table. "Three."

Standing up, I scoop up the weights and walk to stand in front of her. I hang one of the weights. She grunts. After allowing her a moment to get adjusted, I hang another weight. She grunts louder. After hanging the final weight, I run my finger along all four. She squeals.

Giving her a slap, I ask her, "Where's my thank you, slut?"

"Thank you, Sir."

"Want to go for another?"

She hesitates. I know she's up for another orgasm, but does she want another weight pulling on her nipples?

Deciding for her, I say, "Let's go for another."

But first I lube the anal hook. Her body jumps when the tip of it touches her sphincter.

"Now, I know someone has popped this cherry, so there's nothing to be afraid of," I say.

I rub her lower back to relax her before inserting the hook. At the other end of the hook is a rope, which I tie to her head harness to pull her head back toward her ass. I run my fingers over her pussy lips. She shivers, and I hear the weights bumping into each other. Sinking my fingers into her wet heat, I can feel the bulge of the anal hook pressing into her pussy. She makes all kinds of noise while I jam my fingers into her. Some women like it slow and focused. Casey seems to like a harder, faster motion.

After huffing and grunting and wailing, she comes hard. I grab the chair to keep it in place. Her head jerks to the side, which pulls on the anal hook. It's a challenge when you want to give in to the eruptions yet you need to constrain your motions so that you don't inadvertently bring about more pain.

Chapter Four

Casey

I'm in heaven. But how long will this last?

Little bubbles of pleasure continue to pulse to my extremities. He allows me to bathe in the afterglow of my orgasms before removing the weights and unclipping the nipple clamps. Next he removes the gag and harness.

"Thank you, Sir," I make sure to say immediately. I'm surprised at how easy he's gone so far, and I'm appreciative. "Can I do something for you, Sir?"

"Oh, I'm not done with you, princess," he replies.

I knew it. I wonder what's the longest scene he's done? I bet Jack could do a marathon in the world of BDSM.

"Turn around, feet on the chair," he orders.

I comply and watch as he binds my legs in a frog tie, keeping them in their bent position. Spreading my thighs apart, he plays with my clit. I'm already wet for him, and my moisture makes his fingers slide easily over my flesh. Next he picks me up like I weigh nothing at all and flips me upside down before placing me in the chair. My head hangs off the edge of the seat, and my ass rests against the back of the chair where my head would normally be. With more rope, he secures my lower body to the back of the chair so I don't fall off to one side or the other. Finally, he binds my wrists to the hind legs of the chair. It's not a comfortable position, but I love the creativity of it. In this position, he has a full and easy view of my private parts. My clit, cunt, and asshole are his for the taking, like plates on the table. He caresses my bottom and thighs before going over to the wall to pick out an implement. I can't see what he's chosen, but I see the audience members nod their approval. I hear the slice of air and guess it to be the crop or cane. It smacks against my rump. It's the cane.

With the point of the cane, he traces lines across my buttocks. "Last time we had some nice streaks going this way. Tonight we'll have them going this way."

He traces perpendicular lines softly. I brace myself for the contrast, but he only taps the cane lightly against me.

"You been a good girl today, princess?" he asks.

"Yes, Sir," I answer.

"Yeah? What did you do?"

What did I do? What kind of answer is he looking for?

"How were you a good girl?"

I search my brain for what to say and come up with nothing. I can't even say I withheld from masturbating for him.

"I didn't do anything bad," I try.

He snorts and lands the cane sharply on my bottom. "Not the same."

"What kind of good are you looking for? Like volunteering at the food bank type of good or–"

"You're the one who agreed you were a good girl."

He smacks the cane down hard. I cry out.

"Well?" he prompts.

"I texted you to see how the cat was doing."

"That's it? What else did you do today?"

I blush. "I did some reading."

"What kind of reading?"

When I don't answer right away, he strikes me again and again. I grunt each time.

"Erotica," I spit out.

"What else did you do?"

"Surf the web."

"For what?"

"Snowboarding videos."

"Anything else?"

I hesitate, then yelp when the cane bites into me.

"Porn," I mumble.

A few audience members snicker.

"Sounds to me like you were a bad girl, not a good girl. Isn't that right, princess?"

"Yes."

He grabs my toes and pulls them back. Oh no. Just as I fear, he whacks my foot. I cry out. I hate bastinado.

"What kind of porn did you watch?"

He's already made me confess that I watch porn in front of everyone, I've got to provide details too?

He strikes my poor feet several times. I change my mind. I don't like this position.

"BDSM."

"Describe one of the videos you saw."

"It was, um, a story about a thief who break into a woman's home."

He starts playing with my clit. "And?"

"And he ties her up and takes advantage of her."

"Did she like it?"

His fondling is very distracting, and he gets my attention by snapping the cane on my foot.

"Yes and no. Mostly yes," I answer.

"Did you wish you were her?"

"Yes."

"Were you jacking yourself off while you watched?"

"Yes, Sir."

"Another bad girl activity."

The cane lands on my foot, then across my pussy. Just when I start to despair, he starts rubbing my clit again. It's a beautiful ray of sunshine amid the storm of pain before returning to the bastinado. I hate the burst of pain exploding on the bottoms of my feet. He rains the crop relentlessly down on them. I'll take a spanking over bastinado any day. My squeals and cries are loud even to my own ears. I flirt with the idea of using my safe word, but he pauses at that moment. Instead of landing the crop on my feet, he tickles me.

"Oh no, please don't!" I cry between laughs.

I wiggle and strain against the chair. "Stop! Stop it!"

I've always been sensitive to tickling, but on my burning sensitized feet, this is too much.

"You want to go back to the bastinado?" he asks.

No. Yes. I don't know.

My breath is all over the place, and I think I'm about to have the hiccups. Tears, which had pressed against my eyes during the cropping, start to fall.

He returns to spanking the soles of my feet with the cane. Part of me is relieved until the pain starts to build on itself. I whimper in between screams as my tears continue to fall. I can't take much more of this. I'm going to have to use my safe word.

His sense of timing is crazy precise. Pausing the bastinado, he caresses my pussy lips and fondles my clit. I try my best to relish his touch, but I am partially distracted by the fear that he'll go back to the bastinado or the tickling.

To dissuade him from going back to either of those, I ask, "Please, Sir, can I have your cock?"

He sees through me. "Not interested in going back to the bastinado, eh, princess?"

"I'm interested in your cock, Sir," I insist.

"If you thank me for the bastinado, you can have cock."

"Thank you, Sir. Thank you for the bastinado."

From his duffel bag, he pulls out a long dildo and a vibrator. I want to cry out in joy, but I don't want to jinx anything. He rubs the dildo along my folds and clit. Ooh, that feels so good. I want to be done with being upside down and tied in this position, but I want my orgasm.

Turning on the vibrator, he presses it to my clit. Yes! Then he slides the dildo into me. Double yes!

"Good sluts come on demand," he says. "I'm going to count down from ten. Make sure you don't come before then."

Come on demand? Okay, I can do this. I just need to hold off on climaxing. How hard can that be?

He works the dildo in and out of me. My eyes roll toward the back of my head.

Damn, this feels good!

The pressure of the vibrator coupled with the vibrations sends me speeding toward my orgasm.

Wait! He hasn't even started counting yet. I try to pretend like I don't feel anything.

"Remember: you're aiming for the count of one," he tells me.

I concentrate on not feeling anything as he starts the count.

"Ten..."

I try to find something to fix my gaze on, using the advice given on how to better balance on one foot.

Nope. That doesn't work.

"Nine..."

I close my eyes. Picture something gross, like...like...like what? Shit, this feels too good.

"Eight..."

My toes curl. I dig my nails into my palms.

"Seven..."

I dig harder, trying to create enough pain to distract me.

"Six..."

Maybe I can try to move and shift the angle at which the dildo penetrates me to something less effective. But what if I accidentally move the dildo or vibrator to a *more* effective spot? Better to stay still, then.

"Five…"

I tense my body and try to hold in the eruption. I'm almost there!

"Four…"

He moves the vibrator subtly, finding other parts of my clit that are delighted for the stimulation. Oh, shit.

"Three…"

I'm in trouble. Shit, shit, shit.

"Two…"

It's useless. Like trying to plug Old Faithful or keep a volcano from erupting. I scream as my orgasm tears through me. Jolted by the intense euphoria pressing into me, the jerking of my body would have knocked me and the chair down if Jack hadn't been holding it in place somehow. Not that I would have noticed if I had crashed to the floor. My climax would override anything. In fact, the sensation is too much. My body tries to escape the vibrator, still at my clit, but I'm too tightly bound. Only when he removes the vibrator and dildo do I get any relief while my pussy throbs like mad.

"You almost made it, princess," he says, turning off the vibrator and setting the items aside. "What went wrong?"

"Felt too good," I murmur.

Feebly, I lift my head up to see him reach into the duffel bag.

"Well, princess, we're going to have to learn to do better."

I drop my head. I might be in serious trouble.

Chapter Five

Kai

I can tell the position is tiring her, but, to her credit, she hasn't complained or used her safe word. More tears escape her eyes, causing her mascara to run up her face. I check the time on my watch to see how long her head has been hanging off the seat of the chair. I've got time for some more bastinado.

From my bag, I take out rubber bands, which I fit around each of her feet. She looks at them with dread. Squatting down, I wipe some of the tears off her face.

"Think you can do better next time and come only when I tell you to?" I ask her.

"Yes, Sir! Definitely, Sir!

I stand up and pull at one of the bands. "Good. This'll be a little reminder and incentive to help with next time."

I release the rubber band. It snaps into the sole of her foot, causing her to scream.

"Oh my god, that looks painful!" an audience member gasps.

I snap the band on the other foot. Casey screams again. Gently, I run a knuckle along the arch of her foot before reaching for the band again.

"Let's review," I say. "What is it you're going to do?"

"C-Come when you tell me to," she replies.

"And only when I tell you to."

"Yes, Sir."

She howls when I snap the band.

I switch to the other foot. "What else are you going to do to show you're a good sub?"

"Anything you say."

"You're going to be a good girl tomorrow and do what good girls do."

"Okay. Like w-what?"

I snap the rubber band. For a few seconds, she sobs.

"Figure it out," I tell her.

Picking up the vibrator, I turn it back on and hold it to her clit and pussy while I tug on the rubber band.

"P-Please," she gasps.

"Do you need your safe word, princess?"

She remains quiet.

I pull the band more. "Do you?"

She hesitates, then murmurs a weak "no, Sir."

Impressive. I release the band. She lets out a wail. I turn the vibrator up.

"Come nice and good," I instruct.

It takes her a little while to switch from registering pain to registering pleasure. To assist, I sink two fingers into her snatch. She moans. Soon she starts squirming and then convulsing. Removing the vibrator and my fingers, I watch her belly go in and out and the area of her perineum flex.

"One more time," I say and replace the vibrator and sink my fingers back into her hot, wet pussy.

Aided by the adrenaline still in her body, she comes again forcefully. My cock stiffens as her pussy ripples against my fingers. She strains against her bonds and shudders every time my fingers move. I turn off the vibrator and wipe her cum on her bottom before setting aside the vibrator.

The audience applauds as I remove the rubber bands and undo the rope. Scooping Casey into my arms, I sit down in the chair with her in my lap. She appears in a daze, possibly in subspace. I sit quietly with her head against my shoulder. The scene done, the audience turns their attention elsewhere.

"You took your punishment well, princess," I tell Casey as I start to massage her feet.

She sighs, then replies, "I know."

Another minute of silence passes.

"That was..." she begins, "amazing."

Her body no longer feels weak against me, and I eventually set her on her feet. "You can get dressed now."

She does while I wipe down my implements and pack them away.

"I'm going to use the restroom," she tells me. "I'll meet you back at our table."

While I wait for Casey, I review how easy it would be to simply drive her to my place. We could lose her bodyguard or find a convenient way to shoot him. This has got to be the easiest kidnapping job.

A couple approaches me, and the woman asks, "You and your sub into swinging?"

I shake my head. "Not at the moment."

"Let us know if you change your mind."

A man comes up next to ask if I'm a switch. I turn him down too.

Casey returns, sits down, and takes a sip of her tea. "This tastes gross."

"It's shitty tea. Plus, it's cold," I say.

"But you like this stuff?"

"No, I bring my own tea packets. I just ask for hot water."

"So you're like a bona fide tea snob."

I smile. "I can snap those rubber bands harder next time."

She perks up at the words 'next time.'

"We didn't get to do anything for you," she says.

"Yet."

"So when can we?"

"I'll let you know."

She knits her brow, then changes the subject. "So the cat is doing well? She's at your place?"

"Yes."

"You going to keep it?"

"Thinking to. I took her to the vet earlier. There's no microchip and nothing in the local database of missing animals that matches her description."

"Can I see her?"

"When?"

"How about now?"

Sitting back in my chair, I regard her more carefully. Is she interested in the cat or is this her way of prolonging time with me? It doesn't really matter. All that matters is when I plan to pull the trigger on kidnapping her.

"Sure," I say.

She brightens. "We'll take your car?"

"You don't like your driver?"

She tucks a strand of hair behind her ear. "Yeah. Besides, he'll feel like a third wheel."

"Isn't he used to that by now?"

She evades my stare. "When I'm with him, it feels like I have a babysitter. I'm twenty-one years old."

"And still a baby."

She looks at me coyly. "You want to be my daddy again?"

"I don't think you'd want to test my parenting skills," I reply.

"You're wrong about that. I'm pretty adventurous."

"What's adventurous for a rich white girl?"

My sense is that Liam has managed to shelter her from his "business" activities.

"I meant relatively adventurous. In the world of BDSM."

"So not the real world."

She narrows her eyes at me. "You sure you're one to judge, Mister I-drive-a- Bugatti?"

"You forget it wasn't always like this for me."

She leans toward me. "What was it like for you as a kid?"

I don't want to get too personal with her, but until she's secure in my clutches, I don't want to blow her off too much.

"My parents died when I was around four years old. They were walking along the Heihe River when an out-of-control car struck them."

"Oh my god, I'm so sorry."

"My grandparents took care of me until my grandfather passed away, and then my grandmother. So I was on my own as a teen. I supported myself by selling cheap Chinese goods on the other side of the river in Russia. And then I was adopted."

"You were all alone? For how many years?"

"Didn't count. Several. I wasn't always alone. For about a year, I had a dog. It was a stray mutt. We adopted each other."

"Was it love at first sight?"

"Something like that."

She becomes quiet in thought. Wanting to get back to her bodyguard, I ask, "You always have a driver all your life?"

"Not a personal one."

"He with you twenty-four seven?"

"Nowadays."

"You have other drivers or bodyguards?"

"Well, when I'm at home, we have a security guard."

My right-hand man, Andy, has already scoped out the Callaghan residence. There's more than one security guard.

She spots Carmen walking toward us and turns to me. "Wanna blow this popsicle stand?"

We both get up.

"Let me just tell my driver the plan," she says before walking away.

She and Carmen exchange unfriendly looks when they pass each other.

"You're not leaving already?" Carmen asks me.

"I am," I reply.

She wears a bustier that pushes her tits halfway up to her face and snakeskin leggings.

"Bummer. I just got here. You going to be here tomorrow night?"

"No."

"Is that a definite?"

"Yes."

Because I will have kidnapped Casey by then.

Chapter Six

Casey

We pull up to the gates of his beautiful home in Marin County with views of the bay, Golden Gate Bridge, and San Francisco skyline. In his multi-car garage, Jack parks next to the Bugatti.

I'm giddy because this is actually a big step in our non-relationship. Just last night, he seemed done with me. Now he's bringing me home.

"You live alone?" I ask.

"No," he replies.

I wonder who he could be living with? On the drive over, he told me his adoptive father was retired and living with his adoptive mother in the Amalfi Coast. His sister was studying for her master's degree in Paris.

The answer comes running up to Jack when we enter his home. A German Shepherd greets him with several barks and a wagging tail.

"You didn't tell me you had a dog!" I say with delight.

I've wanted a dog since I was two or three years old, but my dad is allergic to dogs in addition to cats. I promised myself I would get a pet after I graduated from college and was on my own.

"Her name's Athena," Jack says as he scratches the back of her neck and receives several licks in the face.

Squatting down, I face the dog and hold out my hand. "Hi, Athena."

She turns to sniff my hand, then licks me too.

"She's friendly," I say.

Jack stares at us. "Not usually."

After I've pet Athena a bit, I ask, "Where's the cat?"

Jack looks to the other side of the foyer where the feline watches us warily from a distance. When he approaches her, she darts away.

"Did you give her a name yet?" I ask.

"No."

We walk into the hallway, but the cat is nowhere in sight.

"I don't think she's settled down yet," he explains.

"I get it."

Just then I hear a door open and shut. Athena starts running that direction.

"Who's that?" I ask.

"Tao. He's my...butler. Want a drink?"

"Sure."

He leads me to a gorgeous room with Brazilian cherrywood flooring and an entire wall of windows overlooking the water. A fire burns in the luxury fireplace that looks like it stretches ten feet wide.

"What would you like?" he asks, heading to a full-size bar.

"Whatever you're having," I reply as I study one of the mixed media art pieces mounted on the wall.

"You don't want what I'm having."

"Well, when you put it like that, I've got to try."

He pours a clear liquid into two porcelain shot glasses. I take one and throw it back. Immediately, a fire flares through my mouth and throat, traveling into my nose, and even my eyes as tears fill my vision.

"Holy crap," I gasp, sounding like I've lost my voice.

He slices a lime and sprinkles sugar on it before handing it to me. I take it, eager to stuff anything in my mouth that might counter the spiciness.

"What is that shit?" I ask when I feel like I have mastery over my mouth again. "That sure as hell isn't tea!"

"It's a liquor from the Guizhou province of China."

"I don't understand why anyone would want to drink that," I say as I watch him calmly down his glass. "I think I'll stick to beer or something sweet like a mojito."

He checks the refrigerator and finds mint. "Mojito it is."

After he's made the drink, he walks toward the sofa in the middle of the room while viewing his cellphone. Following, I sip my drink with joy. It tastes a thousand times better than what I just had. That nuclear shit felt like it was going to burn a hole through my throat.

Having finished texting, he sets his phone down.

"So, you have anything fun planned for tomorrow or do you gotta work?" I ask.

He seems to eye me carefully. "I have some work, but I also might head up to Tahoe. They're expecting snow."

I perk up. "Yeah? I was thinking of going to Tahoe. You ski or snowboard?"

"Both."

No way! He snowboards and is a masterful Dom? How lucky can I get? I want to suggest that we go up together, but that's probably too forward given we barely know each other.

Instead, I ask, "Are you going solo or with friends or...?"

"Solo."

"Then we should meet up when we're both there."

"Maybe."

Aaargh. What's it going to take to get this guy to commit? I finish my drink and set it aside on the coffee table.

His cellphone buzzes. Taking it out, he turns around to view it. I give him a second, then wrap my arms around his waist.

Whipping around, he grabs me by the neck and slams me into the sofa. "Did I say you could touch me?"

His reaction catches me off guard. "Thought you might like to do something since you didn't get to come at the club."

"You don't think I could have if I wanted to? I can do whatever I want with you, princess."

He sounds so ominous, part of me wants to make a run for it. At the same time, the prospect is exciting.

I defer to the second feeling. "That doesn't sound like a bad thing."

"Yeah?" He squeezes my neck harder. "You don't know who you're dealing with."

As I strain to breathe, I tighten my grip on his arm, though I'm no match for his strength. I should cut this out right now, relent, and be a good girl. But, fuck, I want him. We're just playing a game with him pretending to be all mysterious and badass. It's fun.

"Do it," I egg. "I'm not as weak as you think I am."

"You suggesting you can put up a fight?"

"Yes."

He snorts. "This'll be amusing."

With both hands, I pull at his wrist, but his grip is iron.

"Come on, princess. That all you got?" he sneers.

"In a real fight, I'd...claw your face or gouge your eyes," I say while I squirm deliciously beneath his weight.

"Do it," he replies. "Try anything you want."

I try to slap him, but he easily grabs my wrist and pins it to the sofa. He tightens his clasp around my throat. Shit. He's really choking me. What if he doesn't know his own strength?

"I—can't—breathe," I croak.

"Are you having a tough time breathing?" he asks.

I start to panic. For the first time, I worry that our play might be going too far. I need my safe word.

"M-M—" I whisper.

He leans in and places his ear nearer my mouth. "Are you trying to say your safe word, princess?"

I need air! With my free hand, I grab my drinking glass off the table and slam it into his head. The glass shatters. His hold on my throat loosens. I gasp. It takes a moment for the faintness to dissipate and for me to realize that I broke the glass against him. He seems surprised too. Did I hurt him badly?

"I'm sorry," I say.

"Don't apologize," he returns as he shakes shards from his hair, "but that's the end of playing nice."

His hand shoots out and grabs me by the throat again. I'm not sure I want more breath play and try to pry his fingers off while he pulls me up and onto my knees.

"Can we try something else?" I ask.

"Maybe. After you pull down your pants for me."

I undo my jeans and shimmy them down past my hips.

"Panties too," he directs.

I pull down my underwear. Thrusting a hand up my top, he gropes a breast. I had gone without a bra, so he has easy access. Sliding his middle and forefinger around my nipple, he tugs until I wince. Then he jams his fingers between my thighs and pulls them out, wet. He forces his finger into my mouth.

"See how easy this is for me?" he asks before licking the side of my face. Taking one of my hands, he shoves it to my pussy. "Fuck yourself."

I sink two fingers into myself, making sure to rub my clit while I draw my digits in and out. Arousal flames through my veins as I stare into his eyes. There's something menacing there, but I don't know if it's real or just an act.

While still holding my throat in one hand, his other mauls my breasts. I grunt when he slaps the side of one. "You going to come for me?"

"May I, Sir?"

He doesn't answer. Instead, he cups the back of my head with his free hand and presses me face-down into a throw pillow. For a few seconds, I can't breathe, till he backs off.

"Still think you can put up a fight?" he asks.

I manage to lift my face off the pillow. "You wouldn't really hurt me, would you?"

"You can't know for sure, can you?"

He's got a point. Should I just surrender? But I had told him I wasn't weak. What should I do?

Chapter Seven

Kai

I have Casey pinned down on the sofa with her face buried in a pillow, my fingers entangled in her hair, her jeans and panties around her knees. In this position, she's completely helpless. There's nothing she can do, though she tries. I stop pushing her face into the pillow but keep my hand on the back of her head.

"Go ahead," I tell her. "Show me what you got."

"No holds barred?" she asks into the pillow.

"I said you could try anything you want," I reply before pushing her back into the pillow.

There are no more glasses around that she can smash into my head. That part surprised and impressed me. But I've had worse things to the side of my head.

She's not big and strong enough to throw me from her as I sit straddled over her hips. She reaches her hands back to tug at my wrist. Realizing that doesn't work, she tries prying my fingers away. Then she tries scratching me. When the discomfort of having her air cut off makes her more desperate, she digs her nails into my arm and claws away skin.

Since I don't know how much experience she has with asphyxiation, I make sure not to push it. I let her catch a breath while I undo my pants. I've never had reluctance play draw blood before, and Casey's fierceness is turning me on. I pull out my hardened cock and lay myself over her body. She bucks and writhes beneath me. I push her into the pillow again, but not as fully so there's a small amount of air that can get to her, while I reach around her hip with my other hand to find her clit. She stops struggling for a moment.

"That feel good, princess?" I ask, feeling the gush of wetness from her pussy.

Not wanting to wait any longer to sink myself into all that, I spear into her. Damn, she feels good. For a second, I forget myself, consumed only with the amazing heat and wet encasing my cock.

She presses against her forearms in an attempt to lift herself off the pillow, but I maintain the breath play while thrusting deeper and deeper. I release her head. She whips the pillow away and throws it on the floor while drawing in large gulps of air.

Throwing the pillow away doesn't really save her. I let her take in several breaths of oxygen free and clear before clamping my hand over her mouth and nose. She tries to pry my fingers away.

"This could go wrong so easily," I whisper into her ear as I plunge into her harder.

Breath play is dangerous. While I've kept a close eye on her, there's still a risk. I could get unlucky. Only she'd be the one paying the price.

"You get that, don't you, princess?" I ask as I piston my hips more aggressively.

I relax my grip on her face to allow her to answer.

"Yes, Sir. Can I come, Sir?"

I notice her gaze is fixed and intense. "You close to coming?"

"Yes."

Stuffing my fingers into her mouth, I pull her jaw down. "Do it."

"Oh...god..."

I pound away, smacking my pelvis into her backside, as she comes undone. Her body, sandwiched between mine and the sofa, writhes and jerks in limited motions. Closing my eyes, I join her, unleashing the tension wound inside me, spilling it into her. Rapture floods me, shaking my legs and bucking my hips.

Resting atop her, I get my bearings before rolling off her. As I lay on my back, she turns onto her side to look at me.

She grins. "That was fun."

"It's all fun and games until someone gets hurt," I reply.

Shit. I don't know why I said that. It's not my job to parent her, to teach her she can't go around trusting men in crime. One would think her father would have taught her that, especially given his experience.

Casey frowns. "Does everyone in their thirties sound like you?"

"No. They don't fuck like me either."

She smiles again. "That's too bad. I have a thing for older men, thanks to you."

I look at her. "You weren't scared I might actually hurt you?"

"I was. But that's what made it so exciting."

I look at my arm where she scratched me.

"Sorry about that," she says, "but you said I could try anything."

I sit up. "You need better self-defense moves."

She sits up too. "You want to teach me?"

Standing up, I pull up my pants. I could tell her the truth now. That I have no interest in her beyond her use as my pawn and a good fuck. I imagine the look of confusion, followed by anger, then horror or panic when I explain what I mean by her being a pawn. Then I'd have Andy take her and stash her at a safe house. There are several different ones the triad uses.

"That way, I'll put up a better fight when you kidnap me," she adds.

I blink in surprise. She read my mind?

"We're doing it, right?"

The fantasy, I realize.

"If you want, I can dress up like a schoolgirl or a cheerleader," she continues. "Lecherous old men like you always fantasize about doing a young little co-ed, right?"

I snort. "I've never done or had any interest in jailbait, but it sounds like you have a thing for lecherous old men."

She leans against the back of the sofa and slides her hand between her thighs. I watch as she caresses herself.

"You are on the older side of men I've been with," she says. "Second to oldest. I once tried a partner who was thirty-two."

"How many were younger?" I ask. It shouldn't matter, but I want to know the answer.

"Not as many as Carmen would have you believe. Are we talking BDSM partners or everyone, including college and high school?"

"So you lost your virginity in high school?"

"Sweet sixteen."

"Was Daddy okay with that?"

"He didn't know. But he does now." She follows that with an impish grin. "If daddy doesn't like that, then he should punish me. Kidnap me, lock me away, and teach me a really good lesson."

She pins me with her stare while she continues to masturbate. She's a sitting duck right now. But I find myself entertaining the idea of fulfilling her fantasy. Callaghan isn't going to sell the asset for another week, so I can afford another day before she's officially my captive.

Bracing myself against the sofa, I lean over her. "You sure that's what you want, princess?"

She looks at me with large, bright eyes and licks her lips. "Yes, daddy."

With my free hand, I grab her wrist so that she can't touch herself. "From now until when I say you can, you're not allowed to come. You can play with yourself all you want, but you save your orgasms for me."

"Yes, Sir."

"I'll call you with the details."

"What should I wear, Sir?"

"Anything you like. It's all coming off anyway."

She smiles. "Yes, Sir."

Grabbing her by the throat, I pull her to her feet. "You're not going to tell anyone about this, right? I don't want to get in trouble if someone misinterprets what's going on."

"Of course not. I won't tell anyone."

I don't know if I trust her on that, but I am tracking her phone communications. She had to give up her phone while we were at The Lotus. During that time, I had Andy retrieve her phone, break into it, and install an invisible app that tracks her whereabouts, her texts, and her calls.

I ask, "You going anywhere tomorrow?"

"I don't know yet. I kept it open in case I wanted to head up to Tahoe."

"I don't want you going anywhere tomorrow or doing anything except getting yourself ready for me. You can watch your porn or read erotica but nothing else." I jam my fingers between her thighs, where she's dripping with cum. "I want you wet like this, like the slutty little princess you are, when we kidnap you."

"We?"

"Isn't that part of your fantasy?"

"So who else is coming?"

"Men I trust."

"Okay, but I want them to wear condoms. Can we change my safe word?"

"No."

I curl my digits into her cunt. Her lashes flutter. She moans as I stroke her. I work her until she whimpers. She grimaces as her climax nears. I withdraw my fingers and wipe them on her thighs.

"Pull up your pants," I tell her, "and remember: no coming. Mess that up and everything comes off your list of hard limits."

Chapter Eight

Casey

"Sorry you had to wait out here," I say to Chase as I get in the car, which he had parked outside the gates of Jack's home.

"That's my job," he replies as he shifts the car into reverse. He looks through the gates one last time before pulling away. "Sweet mansion. What does this guy do exactly?"

"Sales, I think."

"Of what?"

I shrug. "Fancy cars, buildings, stocks, who knows."

"You gonna see him again?"

My smile could bust my face. "Tomorrow."

"You're really into him."

"And I think he's finally getting into me."

Chase makes it to the end of the driveway and turns onto the street to head home. "Where you guys meeting up?"

I stare at Chase. "You should take the night off. I mean, you don't want to sit in a car for hours again waiting for me."

"As long as there's cell service, I'm good. There's an entire season of *Queer Eye* for me to catch up on."

I frown. Do I tell Chase about the kidnapping plan? I probably have to, otherwise he might think it's real. But I really don't want Chase to be around when it happens. Or maybe I do?

Jack's words echo in my head: *It's all fun and games until someone gets hurt.*

I can't rule out that won't happen. There were a few times with the breath play tonight when I genuinely started to worry. If Jack hadn't released me when he did, I would have been in full panic. So maybe having Chase there wouldn't be a bad idea. I'd have him hide in the background so that his presence won't dampen the mood.

Hugging myself, I can hardly wait for tomorrow night. What I want to do right now is march back into Jack's house and have him get me off. He left me high and dry—correction, wet—and now I'm sitting in squishy underwear. The next twenty-four hours are going to be sooooo long, especially if I can't masturbate. That part is pure evil. Especially given how thirsty I am for him, which I suspect he knows.

I want to know more about him, but it's hard to get past the electricity between us. All I know is he's got bank, is nice to stray cats, and is hella good in bed. So to speak. We haven't actually done it in a bed. A bed's too boring.

When we get back home, I enter the house quietly. It shouldn't be a big deal. I'm twenty-one years old, not sixteen. But my dad doesn't treat me like a grown adult.

I pass by his office on the way to my bedroom and fully expect him to come out and ask me where I've been, then frown when I tell him I haven't been with Kenton. But it sounds like my dad is on a call. I hear what sounds like an Asian language, maybe Japanese or Korean, and then someone speaking English with an accent.

"It's authentic," I hear my dad replying. "And I'm not entertaining extensions. I need to unload this as soon as possible. That's how you know I'm not playing around. Otherwise, I would hold out longer for more money."

Not wanting to know more, I hurry to my bedroom. The best thing about college is that, while I'm at Notre Dame, I can forget about my dad. I still can't believe he wants me to marry Kenton Brady just so he can solidify his "business" with Kenton's father. A cliché mafia marriage. As if we live in feudal times.

I decide to take a shower, and it's *so* hard not to take the showerhead and run the water against my pussy. It's crazy how horny I feel. How am I going to last until tomorrow?

As I lay in bed, I reflect on my good fortune. I didn't have high expectations of my twenty-first birthday being anything special. It's not like I haven't had alcohol prior to turning twenty-one. I've even purchased alcohol before, thanks to the fake ID I got from one of my dad's contacts, which also got me into the casinos at Vegas, so I've done that too. For my birthday, my mom got me a spa package at the Sonoma Mission Inn and Spa as my birthday present, but it's really a gift best suited for her. And my dad thinks he got me the ultimate gift in a husband-to-be.

But Jack. Jack is special. And the best birthday gift I could ever hope for. I love his hard body, strong grip, and smooth skin. That would be enough for most women, but on top of that, he's incredible at BDSM.

Releasing a sigh, I hug my pillow. I actually feel tired and allow myself to drift to sleep.

When I wake up the following morning, the first thing I think about is Jack. I check my phone. There's no text or missed call from him. What if he changes his mind? If he does, I'm not going to wait to hit the slopes. If I go alone, I go alone. I have so much pent-up sexual energy, no amount of time with my vibrator will settle me. Only a hard day on the mountain might.

Laying in bed, I replay last night in my mind. I'm a little sore between the legs from the pounding. If I keep up with Jack, the soreness may never go away. At least, until we stop seeing each other. Winter break feels so short. I have to make the most of my opportunity to be with him.

Just as my hand starts to wander below my belly, a knock at the door startles me.

"Casey."

It's my dad.

"Yeah?" I reply.

"Kenton's parents are thinking to host a dinner tonight and wanted to know if we're available."

Jack told me not to go anywhere, though he wouldn't know if I did. Still, since I don't know when Jack wants to meet up with me, I don't want to take the chance.

"Can we do another night?" I ask. "I'm not feeling so great."

"It's still early in the day. You might feel better later."

"Why don't we do it tomorrow?"

"What if you feel worse tomorrow?"

Ugh. Despite what my dad thinks, a dinner with Kenton isn't going to change my mind about marrying him.

"How about we see how I feel in a few hours?" I try. Hopefully, Jack will have called me by then.

"All right."

I hear my dad walking away. I grab my phone to text to Jack. I'd call him, but there's no phone number associated with his texts.

Awaiting your instructions, Sir.

While I wait for a response, I get up to brush my teeth and wash my face. A video call comes in while I'm brushing my hair. Even though I'd rather not look like I just rolled out of bed, I don't want to miss the call if it's Jack. I pick it up.

"Morning, Sir," I greet when I see it's him.

With his hair perfectly groomed, his smart button-up shirt perfectly pressed, he looks like he's been up for several hours.

"It's almost noon," he replies.

"College circadian rhythms tend to run late, especially when one's having fun the night before. Speaking of fun, we're still on for tonight, right?"

"You alone?"

"Yeah, I'm in my bathroom."

"No one can hear you?"

"Door's closed, and my dad doesn't come in my room without knocking. At least, not since he walked in on me changing years ago. I cried a buttload of tears to make sure he wouldn't do that again. So we good for tonight?"

"Sure."

I breathe a sigh of relief. "So what does daddy want me to do?"

"I want you to be a good girl. Do what good girls do."

"Like what?"

"Figure that out yourself but have an answer for me the next time I call."

"Okay. What else?"

"You already know the part about not coming. Just make sure you stay put until you hear from me."

"Do you have a sense of where and when?"

"I'll let you know later. Just keep your phone on you. And be good."

Wanting to stay on the phone with him longer, I ask, "How's the kitty doing?"

"She's fine."

"What's she doing now?"

"Napping underneath a sofa."

"She still scared?"

"You just worry about yourself, princess."

He hangs up after that. This guy is not talkative at all. I usually like a man of action, but I want more from Jack. Maybe he's standoffish because he wants to make sure our relationship doesn't venture much past sex. I guess I'll take what I can get.

After I've brushed my hair and changed, I go downstairs into the kitchen to see what's for breakfast. Rosita cleans our house and also makes breakfast because my mom's down in Palm Springs, and even if she were here, she doesn't like to cook.

As I help myself to a bowl of fruit salad, my dad walks by.

"Feeling better?" he asks. "You look fine."

He wants me to do dinner with the Bradys, but I don't. What if that's when Jack wants to meet up? My mind starts churning. I don't feel like getting into another big argument with my dad about marrying Kenton. Once I'm back at Notre Dame, there's not much he can do about that and hopefully he'll give up on the idea. But how can I get my dad off my back for today?

"I feel like I might be coming down with something," I say.

"The dinner won't take up that much of your energy," my dad returns.

"I just don't feel up to socializing."

"There's not much socializing. I don't think we'd be the only guests for dinner."

Ugh. I want to tell my dad he should stop trying with the whole Kenton thing.

My dad narrows his eyes. "Maybe you're just tired because you were out late. Where were you?"

"With Chase and his cousin."

"Chase? He's your bodyguard, not your friend. This is not acceptable. I'm going to have to assign you someone else."

Panic shoots up my spine. I do not want another bodyguard. I'm lucky that I formed a rapport with Chase and that we're able to keep each other's secrets. I don't want to have to break in another bodyguard, and I may not be so lucky with a new one.

"Okay," I say hastily. "I won't hang out with Chase anymore. No big deal."

I turn to get orange juice from the refrigerator to buy myself more time to think without my dad trying to read me.

"Why were you hanging out with him in the first place?" he asks.

"He seemed, um, sad because he and his girlfriend got in a fight. We just talked. I gave him advice about women."

I should appease my dad before he gets too far down into the idea of replacing Chase. Jack probably wouldn't want to do the kidnapping in daylight hours, so maybe I can do something with Kenton earlier in the day.

"I was thinking of catching the new Marvel movie with Hannah," I say. "Maybe I can invite Kenton instead of going to dinner with his folks. If I am coming down with something, I'd rather stay in during the evening hours."

That seems to satisfy my dad. "Are you definitely going to the movies?"

"I'll go text Kenton right now."

Taking my fruit and juice with me, I head back to my bedroom. My phone was actually in my pants pocket the whole time, but I wanted to get away from my dad.

I decide to text the group about going to the movies this afternoon. I don't want to go alone with Kenton.

Hannah asks why not catch an evening show. I reply that I'm bored right now. She, Kenton, and his cousin Aiden text back that they're willing to go.

After we've finalized the details of meeting up, I think about Jack's instructions to stay put until he calls again. But why should it matter if I go out for a little bit? I can still be a good girl.

Besides, he won't know.

Chapter Nine

Kai

Watching a livestream from Casey's phone of the text messages she's sending to her friends on my phone, I shake my head.

"That's not being a good girl," I murmur.

There's a risk that she'll tell one of her friends about the kidnapping. It doesn't bother me if she does unless that friend interferes with my plans.

"You're doing the kidnapping tonight?" Andrian asks me on a call later while I'm outside with Athena.

I throw her fetch toy across the lawn, then check my phone. Without Casey knowing, her phone is sharing its location with mine. I can see that she's at a movie theater in the Marina. I get confirmation from my guy, who's still tailing her.

"Yes," I reply. I'm actually looking forward to it.

"We've hacked into Callaghan's video calling app. He had calls with Pakistan and North Korea last night. The auction is moving forward. People are interested, but they are also hesitant because they've never heard of this Callaghan before."

"And because of that, they won't offer top dollar. We could see if he'd be willing to cut a deal with us. I could sell the asset for four or five times what he can get."

"After we get the girl, no?"

"Of course."

"I don't want to give that *svoloch'* one fucking dollar."

"The money doesn't bother me. Pay him, don't pay him. As long as he ends up dead."

"But not an easy death, yes? We shoot his family while he watches."

I don't respond. I'm not one for gratuitous or extraneous deaths. There are members in the triad who are like Andrian, but I prefer not to involve innocents when possible. But a statement needs to be made. You don't steal my shit and get away with it.

But is Casey an innocent? It doesn't seem like she's involved with her dad's line of work, but I don't know that for certain. If she's involved by more than association, then she's part of the enemy. But if she's not, how do I feel about killing her?

There are other ways to make Callaghan feel the pain. Killing Casey isn't the only option. If I want, I can get Andrian to see that. He and I are usually on the same page, even if we don't start out that way. In our days working the streets of Blagoveshchensk as teenagers, we were always in sync.

We met when I was getting the shit beat out of me by a couple of Russian boys when I refused to hand over the cheap electronics I had brought over from Heihe to sell in Russia. Andrian and his friend, Puskin, intervened. Because I was good at acquiring the goods in Heihe, Andrian proposed a partnership. At one point, Puskin wanted a bigger cut—out of my half. Andrian kicked Puskin out of the partnership, so it became the two of us for a few years.

"We can discuss what's necessary later," I tell Andrian as Athena returns with her stick toy and drops it at my feet. I pick it up and throw it again. I'm still surprised that Athena accepted Casey as quickly as she did. Usually, Athena is guarded and skeptical of strangers. And she remains wary of some people, including Andrian, whom I consider my best friend.

After hanging up with Andrian, I call Casey, even though I know she's in the movie. The call goes straight to voicemail, so her phone must be off. Again, I shake my head. She didn't follow my instructions about keeping her phone on. There will be a price to pay for that, on top of her punishment for disobeying me about not going anywhere.

I toy with what manner of consequence I could impose. More bastinado. Hours of orgasm denial. A heavy whipping with the single tail.

All of the above.

Athena nudges me. Lost in thought, I didn't notice she had already brought back her stick for me to throw again. I pick it up and notice it's time to get her a new fetch toy yet again.

But her ears perk up. She's heard something. She barks, announcing Andy's approach.

"Vu will be the third guy if you want him," Andy tells me, "though his kid's supposed to visit this week."

Vu's divorced, and his young son lives with the mother in Fresno.

"No," I say. "He should see his kid. Let's go with Antonne."

"So it'll be your two bodyguards, Antonne and Tao, plus Jay."

Jay is the specialist in kidnapping I brought in. With me as the fourth, Casey should get a decent gangbang.

"Unless you want in on the fun?" I ask.

"I'll hold the fort for you here, boss, and meet up with you later."

I nod and toss the stick for Athena while I review what will happen after I kidnap Casey. The plan is to take her to a cabin the triad owns in Nevada County near the quieter side of Lake Tahoe. Once she's safely in my hands, I'll inform Callaghan that we have his daughter. Any attempt to unload the asset will mean she dies. We'll know then how much Liam loves his daughter.

If he doesn't negotiate, we'll look to retrieve the laptop in other ways. Andy is feeling out whether or not anyone on Liam's payroll can be bribed into shedding light on where the laptop might be stashed. It may or may not be in the Callaghan residence at the moment. We also have plans to break into the home of Scott Magee, whom we've identified as Callaghan's right-hand man, and see if the asset is there. Either way, we take Magee and get him to tell us what he knows. Andrian wanted to execute the break-in last night, but I didn't want to tip our hand to Callaghan until I had Casey.

After I'm done playing with Athena, I head back inside my house. The cat Casey and I discovered on our first "non-date" has been watching us warily from the patio door. She follows Athena.

I check on Casey's whereabout. Though her phone is off, my guy texts that she left the movie theater. He informs me when she is back home. Shortly thereafter, her phone comes back online. I video call her from my office. When she picks up, I see that she's in her bedroom.

"I told you to have your phone on," I say.

"I know. I'm so sorry," she replies. "I didn't realize the battery had run down."

"Your phone's been dead for several hours."

"I took a nap. You tried to call?"

I eye her off-the-shoulder sweater and dangling earrings. "You're dressed up for a nap."

Her sapphire blue eyes show some worry. "Our maid hasn't done the laundry yet, so I just grabbed the first thing I saw."

That doesn't explain the earrings, but I allow the lie. For now.

"I'm really, really sorry I let the phone die," Casey apologizes. "It won't happen again."

"It better not. Or I might think you're having second thoughts."

"No! Definitely not. I'm on."

"What else were you doing this afternoon?"

"Um, reading."

"What were you reading?"

"Random, naughty stuff online."

She's a pretty good liar. Has probably had a good amount of practice in her life. I ask, "What kind of naughty stuff?"

"Stories with dubcon and noncon."

"You like that stuff?"

"Yeah. I think we secretly all do. I bet even men fantasize about not having control. There's nothing wrong with fantasies. Doesn't mean I want it to happen in real life. I mean, in real life, if some gross, creepy old perv twice my age groped me without my permission, I'd want to fry his balls."

"Would you really?" I challenge.

She bristles. "I wouldn't do nothing."

"It happens all the time."

She raises a manicured brow at me. "You know through experience?"

"I don't have to grope women without their consent. They come onto me. Like you did."

She blushes. It's cute.

"But I see it happen all the time. Especially from men with power and money. And the most I've seen a woman do is walk away. Usually, she suffers the discomfort in silence. Some even return an awkward smile."

"They probably didn't want to make a scene. I would."

Studying her, I'm not sure. She sounds convinced, but reality doesn't always play out the way one thinks it will.

"Ever made a scene?" I ask. "I bet you've been groped at least once at a frat party or bar."

"There aren't any fraternities at ND, though there are plenty of parties, especially in the guys' dorms and off campus. And, yeah, it's happened. It was usually too dark to see which asshole actually did it. But if *you* want to grope me, I'm all for it."

"I'll grope you, princess, and then some."

She lights up. "You better. So when is this happening?"

"I'll let you know. For now, I want to make sure you're prepped for tonight. Reading naughty erotica is a good start. Did you jack off while you were reading?"

"No."

"Do you usually?"

She lowers her lashes briefly before responding, "Yes."

"Show me."

"You want me to masturbate in front of you?"

I lean back in my chair. "Or sing and dance. You choose, but there is a right choice and a wrong choice."

"I know the right choice, Sir."

She props her phone on a dresser or vanity top before sitting down in her chair and adjusting the angle of the phone so that I can see most of her.

"Sometimes I start by touching myself," she says, grabbing a tit through her shirt.

She changed out of her earlier outfit and is now in a cropped tee with sweatpants. I can tell she's not wearing a bra even before she pulls up her shirt to play with her nipples. They harden quickly. I feel warmth percolating in my loins. I don't always respond this quickly to the simple sight of breasts, but Casey's gotten under my skin a bit.

Now she has her other hand in her sweats. She slumps in her chair and starts getting into the performance, parting her lips, pouting, moaning.

I adjust my crotch. "You do anything else?"

"I've got some toys I usually use."

"Let's see them."

She gets up, goes to a nightstand, and pulls out two vibrators, one smaller and lipstick shaped, the other a larger pink rabbit.

Holding up the smaller one, she says, "This one is quieter. The rabbit is waterproof. I use it in the bath."

"Start with the quieter one," I say, though I know she's mostly in the house alone except for her bodyguard and possibly one other security guard. The man I have tailing Callaghan told me Casey's dad left the house for his office in the Marina. I considered having my men jump Callaghan there, but his office is on a busy street with restaurants and shops that stay open late.

She pulls her sweats and panties down and opens her legs, giving me a nice view of her cunt. Nestling the vibrator at her clit, she turns it on. Her eyes close momentarily as she sinks into the pleasurable vibrations.

"That feel good?" I ask.

"Yes, Sir."

I let her enjoy her vibrator for several minutes before asking, "What was the naughtiest story you were reading?"

While thinking, she parts her pussy lips so she can get more of the vibrator against her clit. "I read one about a woman who likes sucking cock through glory holes."

"Would you like to do that?"

"If you want me to, Sir."

I think she's just playing along, though I happen to know a triad member who runs a sex club with glory holes.

"When I kidnap you, you're at my mercy. I could make you work some glory holes."

At my suggestion, she moans. "Would you really do that, Sir?"

"Sure. A lot of men would pay a pretty penny to get sucked off by a slut like you."

"You'd pimp me out to other men?"

"That turns you on, doesn't it?"

Her brow furrows. "Can I come, Sir?"

"You know the answer to that."

Frowning, she moves the vibrator away.

"Use the other one now," I command.

Setting aside the smaller vibrator, she picks up the rabbit and slowly slides it into her wet slit till the ears hug her clit. She takes in a shaking breath.

"Turn it on," I tell her.

Bracing herself, she flips the switch to on. "What happens if I accidentally come, Sir?"

"I'll stick you in a reverse glory hole."

"How do those work?"

"I stick your body through a larger hole in the wall. Half of you is on one side of the wall. The other half of you is available for anyone to use."

She groans.

"You could be bent over with your ass facing out," I continue. "Or you could lie on your back on a built-in platform, your legs forced apart and tied to the wall."

"You seem to know a lot about these glory holes."

"Yeah."

"You ever avail yourself of one?"

"I like to know the pussy I'm pounding. But you, dirty little slut that you are, you'd like being a hole in the wall, wouldn't you?"

She bites down on her lower lip.

"Getting banged by a line of men whose faces you can't see," I say.

"Maybe I could blow you while I'm getting fucked on the other side," she murmurs.

Shit. My boner stretches against my pants.

"Unless you'd rather be on the other side?" she asks impishly.

That's a tough choice. I picture myself drilling into her from behind, maybe reaching a hand through the hole to squeeze her breast or pull her nipple. But getting a blowjob while another cock fills her pussy is arousing too.

"Please, can I come, Sir?" she begs.

"Don't even ask," I admonish.

Her breaths are short, her brows knit. She turns off the vibrator.

"Princess looks so sad without her orgasm," I observe of her distressed countenance. "Let's go back to the other vibrator."

She makes the switch. Shortly into the new set of vibrations, she starts to squirm.

"I can't," she says, turning off the vibrator. She slumps further in the chair and runs a hand through her hair.

"All right, you can put away your toys and go back to reading your naughty erotica. I'll call you later."

"Call me soon, Sir."

"Remember to be a good girl."

I end the call, which amused and turned me on more than I expected. Her enthusiasm and arousal are rubbing off on me.

But this is supposed to be a job. I've never mixed play with work before. As long as it's just play and nothing more, I should be fine.

Chapter Ten

Casey

After hanging up with Jack, I press my lips into a grim line. I really, *really* want to jam one of my vibrators back against my clit. I could come in a minute. He wouldn't know, right? But I've already broken one of his rules. Do I want to push it?

He seemed to buy my lie about taking a nap and didn't seem too bothered that I didn't have my phone on. But Jack doesn't seem like the kind of guy who lets things slide. Then again, it's not like I know him well.

So what should I do?

I want to do what he says, to have the full experience. By not coming now, my orgasm later could be cataclysmic.

Drawing in a deep breath, I stand up, grab my vibrators, and take them to the bathroom to cleanse them.

I can do this.

Putting the vibrators back in their drawer, I stare at them, tempting me like a chocolate lava cake might tempt a chocoholic. I shut the drawer and consider pulling out a cigarette. But Jack's last words to me was to be a good girl. He doesn't smoke, so he might not approve of smoking. Maybe I can get away with just one? What's the worst that can happen if he did manage to smell the smoke on me? He'd punish me, and that's not necessarily a bad thing.

But part of me wants to succeed in this challenge, to see if I have the willpower. So what does being a good girl entail besides denying myself an orgasm? I need something else to take my mind off sex or I'll go crazy not being able to come. What else would a good girl do?

There's the non-sexual definition of a good girl, I suppose. Like working in a soup kitchen or something. But I'm not supposed to go out. I could make a charitable donation. That's something easy, doesn't take much time or require me to exert myself in any way.

Grabbing my laptop, I flop on the bed and search for charities, but that pulls up a wide variety of options from the United Nations stuff on saving the pandas. I want something more specific to me. I think for a bit, then add the word 'girls.' There's a lot there too, including issues I wasn't really aware of, like child marriage and fistula. I had to look up what fistula was. Though all the organizations that popped up sounded like they did good work, nothing jumped out at me.

Though I don't expect to find anything, I add the word 'snowboard.' I come across a nonprofit that volunteers to bring disabled and underprivileged kids to the slopes and teach them how to ski or snowboard. I read through their whole website. It sounds like a cool group. I make a donation. It's the first one I've made outside of school-related fundraisers, unless one counts buying Girl Scout cookies.

It never occurred to me that many winter sports aren't as accessible. With skiing or snowboarding, there's gear to rent and lift tickets to buy, all of which is more expensive than finding an open field and purchasing a soccer ball or baseball bat.

Noticing the organization is also seeking volunteers, I fill out their online form. Now what?

I decide to search the internet for more about Jack. I really should learn more about him. But the internet doesn't yield much, partly because I don't have a lot to go on. I end up wandering over to some erotica sites since that's what I told Jack I had been doing. He may or may not quiz me later on what I've read. Reading taboo stories, however, stirs my libido. Just as my hand starts sliding between my thighs, there's a knock at my door. I quickly close my laptop.

"Casey."

It's my dad.

I open the door. I can't wait until I'm done with college and have my own place.

"How was the movie?" he asks.

"Good," I reply.

"You didn't want to hang out with Kenton and your friends longer?"

"Like I said, I'm not feeling all that great. Hope I'm not coming down with anything because I'd like to get some shredding in before going back to school."

"Maybe you, Kenton, and your friends can all go together. I can see about getting you guys a cabin."

I pause. Getting a cabin would be great. Hanging out with Kenton would be a no. But I want to end this conversation with my dad sooner rather than later.

"Sure," I end up saying.

"Also, have you noticed anything out of the ordinary when you're out?"

"Like what?"

"Like you're being followed."

"No."

"Mikey noticed a new car parked down the block."

I stare at my dad. Mikey is one of my dad's security guards.

"He keeps tabs on every car?" I ask, incredulous.

"He noticed it was there yesterday too."

"Maybe one of the neighbors has a new bae visiting."

"Maybe. Just be aware of your surroundings when you're going out. Probably good if you stay in, especially since you're not feeling well."

"Okay."

"I'm going to check with Chase to see if he's noticed anything unusual."

My pulse ticks up a few beats, but I'm pretty sure Chase won't snitch on me.

"I'll be at the office late," my dad says.

After he leaves, I hop on my bed. Jack didn't give me any idea when he would call back. I hope it's soon. I'm bursting at the seams waiting around. The only part I'm a little nervous about are his friends. I don't think Jack's social circle would intersect with my dad's, but that would be the only issue.

Jack wants me wet for the kidnapping. That won't be hard. I just have to imagine all the naughty things Jack might do to me. Did he say how many friends he was bringing? Am I really doing this? I wonder what Aleisha would think of this and if it was going too far?

Hannah would probably think so, though she's pretty dirty-minded herself. She reads as much erotica as I do. The difference is she doesn't have the guts to actually do much. She has a low pain threshold and would fall to pieces if she broke a nail. But she's told me one of her wet dreams involved being trapped in the locker room of the football team and having sex with the lead running back and one of the wide receivers at the same time.

How often does one get to live out their fantasy? An opportunity like this doesn't grow on trees. I once thought about being an actor because role-playing and pretending to be someone else sounds fun. This kidnapping is going to be *hella* fun.

Laying on my bed, I picture the hot and heavy sex Jack and I might have in the back of a car or van. I *really* want to take out my vibrator and come. Jack will never know if I did, and I'm pretty good at lying. But I also want to follow his instructions truthfully.

I take several deep breaths to try and calm my ardor. When is he going to call, dammit?

Our housekeeper probably made dinner before she left, so I decide to wander into the kitchen to see what I can eat. There's a lasagna in the oven. Though I'm too excited to have much of an appetite, I make myself eat just to pass the time and because I don't want to be hungry halfway through the kidnapping.

Jack doesn't call until it's past ten o'clock at night. I'm not sure when my dad will be coming back, and I'd rather not be walking out the door if he's home.

"Finally!" I say when I pick up Jack's call.

"Put on your earbuds," he instructs.

I do as he says. My pulse races.

"You alone?" he asks.

"Yeah. My dad's at his office."

"What did you tell him?"

"About what?"

"About where you're going to be tonight."

"Nothing yet," I answer. "He might just think I've turned in early."

"Leave him a note that you'll be staying over at a friend's house."

"So this is an overnight kidnapping?"

"I'm only doing this once, so we might as well make the most of it."

My excitement soars, as does my nervousness. "I'll text my dad that I'm at Aleisha's. He won't know how to get ahold of her."

"A note is better. That way you don't have to deal with potentially nosy questions."

"Good idea."

"There's a liquor store outside Colma called JJ's Liquors," Jack continues. "Take the 12:06 BART train from Van Ness to Colma, then get a cab to the store. You won't need your driver."

"Yes, Sir."

"If you're not there, I'll assume you changed your mind. In which case, this is goodbye."

"I'll be there," I assure him.

"Will you?"

"Yes!"

"I don't like setting things up for a no-show."

"I'll be there," I insist.

"Then I'll see you in two hours."

After hanging up, I go find Chase in the break room designated for dad's staff and bring him up to speed.

"You sure about this?" Chase asks. "Didn't you meet this guy for the first time just the other day?"

"That's what you're for," I reply. "You can follow me onto the BART train, then catch your own cab to the liquor store."

"Then what? I'm going to have the cab follow you?"

"Why not?"

He looks at his watch. "If I drive down to Colma now, I can leave the car at the train station and catch the train back to Van Ness to meet up with you. That way I don't have to deal with a cab driver who might find what we're doing a bit suspicious, which it is. What do you know about this Jack guy anyway? And he's bringing friends? Who are his friends? How long is this going to last? The more I think about it, the more I don't like this whole thing."

"It's just going to be a few hours."

"What if your dad doesn't approve overtime for this?"

"I'll find a way to pay you. I promise."

Chase runs his hand through his hair several times. "I don't know. I'm already kind of tired."

"I'll make you some coffee. Please. I promise I won't ask you for any other special accommodations. I'm thinking to go to Tahoe for the rest of winter break. Maybe I can find a rental with an in-law unit where you and your bae can stay. You can't really watch me when I'm on the slopes, so you guys can have your own fun."

He hesitates. "Fine. You owe me a favor."

I throw my arms around him. "You're the best!"

I start the coffee machine.

"You sure you're not in over your head?" Chase asks.

"What are you so worried about?" I return as I rummage through the refrigerator for something to snack on.

"You're going to let a guy you just met kidnap you?"

"What are you worried he's going to do to me?"

"Maybe he's secretly a sex trafficker."

Finding nothing that catches my eye, I decide to toast a slice of sourdough. "A guy as rich as he is?"

"Men of wealth and power do shitty stuff all the time. Don't you pay attention to the news? I don't know. Something about this guy feels off."

I pause to consider Chase's words. Jack is unlike anyone I've ever met before.

"He's just aloof and a little intense," I say.

"I'm not talking about his demeanor, though there's that too. I was just thinking about how I couldn't get ahold of you that night you went to his club. And I could have sworn one of security guards walking the grounds of his home had an assault rifle."

"So?"

"That's a lot of heat for a home security guard."

I spread butter on the toast. "Maybe he's paranoid, like Dad."

"But your dad has reason to be paranoid. What's Jack's excuse?"

I shrug my shoulders. I don't really care if Jack is paranoid. He's the most amazing BDSM player I've ever come across, and I'm not letting this opportunity slip away. Besides, Chase only thinks he saw some assault gun. He's not sure.

Chase takes his coffee to go so that he can park the car at the Colma BART station, then make it back on time to follow me onto the train. I finish my coffee, then go upstairs to change.

Time to *carpe diem.*

Chapter Eleven

Kai

"The bodyguard went on the train with her," one of my men texts to me and Andy.

We're sitting in his car across from JJ's Liquors, a business owned by the triad as a front for a lot of activities. It doesn't have a license to operate past midnight, so it's closed, though there are a few lights on inside. There are no customers, and the only other vehicle in the parking lot is the cargo van with Antonne, Tao, and Jay.

I turn to Andy. "Take care of the guy."

Andy responds with only a nod, which is all I need from him. I don't need the details of how Andy plans to do it because I trust him. Even though he's only twenty-six, what he lacks in experience, he makes up for in brains. The guy probably could have gotten a PhD from MIT if he hadn't gotten into the triad.

Our next update is that Casey and her bodyguard have arrived at the Colma BART Station. Casey gets into the taxi we had planted just for her. The triad runs a taxi company too, one of many legitimate businesses that we run to clean our money. Her bodyguard gets into his own car.

"Probably planted it," Andy tells me, "after Casey told him the plan."

"Convenient," I say, glad he isn't grabbing a cab. The fewer witnesses and collateral victims the better.

Not much later, I see a cab pull in and drop Casey off at the front of the store before departing. She wears a trench coat over what appears to be thigh high boots. I notice her bodyguard pulling into the parking lot. Tao gets out of the van to approach Casey. He asks her a question. She follows him toward the van. When she reaches the back, he pushes her in. Jay is there and throws a hood over her head. I watch the bodyguard stir but remain behind the wheel. Andy screws the suppressor onto his .45 ACP.

"I'll be back," he tells me as he gets out of the car and walks toward the bodyguard.

Casey is now in the van with the doors closed. She won't be able to see or hear much.

Andy knocks on the driver-side window of the car. When the bodyguard lowers the window, Andy pulls out his handgun and shoots. The bodyguard's body lurches to the passenger side from the force of the shot. Andy reaches in and turns off the engine.

After Andy returns, he says, "Vu's at the BART station. I'll pick him up and dispose of the bodyguard."

I get out of the car.

"Have fun," Andy says.

I walk to the van and get into the passenger seat. Tao is at the wheel and starts the van. I glance into the back and see that Casey is sitting on the floor with the hood over her head and a gag in her mouth, her hands tied behind her back and her ankles bound together with rope. Her purse and phone, which Antonne has already turned off, lay next to her

Tao drives toward the freeway. Casey makes a half-ass attempt to get out of her bonds while protesting through her gag. My men are quiet on the drive toward Tahoe. About thirty minutes in, Casey appears to get anxious. Her struggles intensify. She starts kicking.

"Hey!" Antonne barks. "None of that or we hurt you bad, bitch."

She stops. I wonder if she's scared now. The drive to the north end of Lake Tahoe takes more than two and a half hours. Halfway there, she tries to talk through the gag. It sounds like she's asking for me. I consider pulling off the side of the road to have some fun, but I don't want some CHP pulling up to check on us.

Casey gets more desperate, trying harder to free herself from the bonds.

"Behave yourself," I tell her.

The sound of my voice seems to settle her. For the rest of the ride, she remains still and quiet. We arrive at a three-story cabin nestled in a densely wooded area in Nevada County, the entire population of which is less than half the City of Oakland. There's no one within miles, though the town of Truckee and the ski resorts aren't too far.

Casey tries to talk. I nod to Jay, who removes the gag.

"Finally!" she exclaims. "That was a hella long drive. Where the fuck are we?"

"That's not important," Jay replies.

Tao gets out of the driver seat and into the back of the van.

"Jack?" Casey asks.

"Let's see what's under the coat," Tao says, reaching for the tie at the waist.

She shirks away when she feels the tug, but Jay grabs her, keeping her in place. Tao successfully loosens the tie and undoes the buttons.

"Jack!" she tries again.

I could probably reassure her, but she might have more fun being scared.

"Damn, look at this," Tao says after he's pulled open her coat to reveal a red plaid skirt and a cropped white top with a cropped sweater vest.

"Sexy schoolgirl," Jay remarks.

"You mean a school-slut," Antonne corrects. "I bet she doesn't even have panties under that short little skirt."

He lifts up her skirt. She does have panties. Lacy red ones. He rubs her through the fabric.

"Did Jack say you could touch me?" she demands.

"Jack said we could do whatever we wanted with you, cupcake."

"Don't call me that."

"You prefer 'whore' instead?"

"No."

"Too bad." Antonne turns to Tao and Jay. "What should we do with the whore first?"

"Have her suck dick, of course," Jay answers.

"Yeah," Tao seconds enthusiastically. He's told me before that his wife is mediocre at giving head.

"Should we take the hood off her?"

"Nah, we just need to cut a hole." Tao whips out his knife. "Don't move unless you want to get cut in the face."

Casey stills while Tao pulls the fabric of the hood and slices it, creating an opening for her mouth.

She searches for me. "Jack?"

Hearing the worry in her voice, I decide to speak. "Do what the nice man says, princess."

She relaxes. "These guys have condoms, right?"

"Maybe," I reply, deliberately putting her on edge so that she can see what a vulnerable situation she has walked herself into.

Antonne pulls out packets of condoms and hands one to Tao. Even if she hadn't specifically requested condoms, my men aren't allowed to come in her. That's reserved for me.

Tao drops his pants, gets his condom on first, and positions himself in front of Casey, who struggles against Jay's grip on her.

"Does he have a condom on?" she asks. "I just don't want to catch anything."

"If that was so important to you, you shouldn't have asked to be kidnapped," I tell her.

Tao places his cock at her lips. When she resists, he pinches her nose through the hood, cutting off her air. When she opens her mouth to breathe, he slams himself in. Not ready for how far he'd shove into her, she gags. Tao continues to hold onto her nose as she struggles harder against Jay.

"Relax," I command.

When she does, she seems to realize that Tao does have a condom on and becomes more compliant, wrapping her lips about Tao's cock.

"That's better," he says, pressing his hips at her.

Jay pulls up her crop shirt and sweater to reveal her matching satin and lace bra. "Look at this. Our little schoolgirl is a slut."

"I'll fuck the slut out of her," Antonne says.

Tao lets Antonne have a turn. Jay mauls her tit. With the hood over her head, I can't tell if she's having a good time, but she hasn't used her safe word.

"I bet she's liking this," Tao says, stroking himself to keep his cock hard.

Jay shoves his hand into her panties. "Yep, she's wet as a fish."

Antonne grabs her hair through the hood. "A slut like you should be able to take me deeper."

Her body heaves as it tries to distance itself from Antonne's penetration, but with Jay holding her, his stocky body a wall against her back, she can't escape. After a minute, I wave Antonne off to give her a break from choking. Tao replaces Antonne.

"I wanna come on her tits," he says as he cups the back of her head to maneuver her up and down his shaft.

Jay pulls up her clothes. Pulling out of her mouth, Tao jerks himself till his cum splatters onto her chest. He exchanges spots with Antonne.

"Suck me good and I won't try to choke you with my dick," Antonne tells her.

I shake my head, half amused that my security detail is getting into this, as if they're auditioning to be porn actors.

Casey goes down on Antonne in earnest, sucking like her life depended on it.

"Holy shit," Antonne murmurs. He doesn't last long and comes over chest and torso.

"You're welcome," Jay tells Tao and Antonne before pushing Casey down.

While she lies on her back, he straddles her head and pulls out his cock. After putting on the condom, he braces an arm against the floor of the van and slides himself into her mouth.

Tao pulls her panties down past her hips. "Look at this. She trimmed herself."

He runs his fingers through her pubes. Antonne does the same, then pries her thighs apart to rub her pussy. Tao moves to her tits, pulling them out of her bra.

"Not bad," Tao says. "I like them bigger, though."

"Your wife has crazy big tits," Antonne says.

"They look extra big because she's Vietnamese, and all the women are like petite, you know? I think I might pay to have her tits augmented a second time."

Antonne sinks a finger into Casey's snatch. Jay pumps his hips up and down until he reaches his climax, spilling his seed onto the hood.

After Jay gets off of her, Casey turns onto her side. "Jack?"

"Still here, princess," I answer.

My men pull their pants up, then hop out of the van. Jay goes to check the cabin. I squat down next to Casey and observe the cum dripping down from a tit, her panties still around her knees.

"How was that?" I ask her.

She doesn't say anything at first, and I wonder if my men went too hard on her.

"Fucking amazing," she answers.

I release a breath and smile.

"Your friends are really good with the dirty talk," she adds. "But where are we? Why the fucking long drive? I've been needing to pee for the past, like, forty minutes."

"Poor princess needs to pee?"

"Yes! Are we near a bathroom?"

"Yes, but you've got to hold it a little longer."

"Why?"

I give her a wicked grin even though she can't see me. "Because I said so."

I run my fingers through her pubic hair. She shivers. I trail a digit over her clitoris. She moans. I curl the finger into her pussy. She exhales. Gently, I press and pull the finger.

"Did you come today?" I inquire.

"No, Sir."

I think she's telling the truth.

"I've been really good," she says. "I even did something charitable. I made a donation and signed up to volunteer."

This surprises me. "Did you?"

"It's this nonprofit that works with disadvantaged kids. You can't do much more good than that, right?"

"Not bad for a princess. It almost balances out the bad you did."

"The what?"

"You didn't follow all my instructions, did you?"

I withdraw my finger.

"What do you mean?" she asks.

Jay returns. "Cabin's good."

I get out of the van. Tao and Antonne pick up Casey and carry her into the cabin, down to the basement.

"Boss, can we get more perks like this more often?" Jay asks as I head into the cabin.

I give him a stare that makes him crawl back into his shell. I probably should be nicer to a man who's supposed to take a bullet for me, but I compensate my security detail well. For some reason, I'm feeling a little irritable. Maybe it's because I'm the only guy who hasn't come on Casey, though that will be rectified soon enough. It turned me on to see her blow three men, but part of me felt off about it. I'm not sure why. After all, Casey liked it.

And there's plenty more where that came from.

Chapter Twelve

Casey

The long boring ride while tied up and breathing in a hood was bad enough, but now I seriously need to pee. I was distracted from nature's call when Jack's friends started messing with me. It was a fantasy come true. Getting used like that by three different men felt so dirty and fun. But did Jack do nothing but watch? I remember feeling hands on my body, but I couldn't tell if they were Jack or not.

Now I'm being carried somewhere. Chase is not going to be happy that he had to follow us for what felt like two or maybe even three hours. He's probably feeling either pissed or concerned. Or both.

I made the assumption that maybe Jack would take me back to his place, but now I see I should have confirmed that. It's a good thing I left that note telling my dad I'd be at Aleisha's. He might not be happy, but I'm an adult. I should be able to crash wherever I want. I wish I had my own place to stay at when I'm on break from ND, then I could really come and go as I please.

We're going down a set of stairs, but I can't see anything through this hood except that a light has turned on. I'm dumped onto a table or something. No. It doesn't feel like the surface of a table. And it's not sturdy. There's a slight swaying sensation. Plus, I can't stretch my legs out because my feet keep bumping into...bars?

I call out, "Jack?"

I shift my body. My hands, still pinioned behind my back, graze steel bars. Am I in a cage?

I hear the clang of something above me, and the snap of a lock. I'm pretty sure I'm in a cage. Holy crap. My pulse ticks up. This could be either really cool or really bad. I can trust Jack, right?

"I wouldn't," he says when I try to sit up fully. "It's not a very tall cage."

I do it anyway and bump my head on the top of the cage. "But I need to use the bathroom!"

"How badly?"

"Bad!"

I hear one of Jack's friends snicker and another mutter, "Oh, damn, sucks to be her."

I hear them leave, the sound of a door closing, and footsteps going up the stairs. I presume I'm alone with Jack. I hope I am. As fun as his friends were, I mainly want to be with him.

"Lie on your side," Jack directs.

I do as he says. I feel his hand on my thigh and sigh. This is what I've been waiting for all day long. He caresses my ass beneath my short skirt before sliding between my legs. His hand glides against flesh. Should I remind him that I really need to pee? But I don't want him to stop what he's doing.

"Does that make it feel better?" he asks.

"Yes, Sir," I reply, relishing the way his fingers rub against me.

"Your panties are drenched. Must have been hard for you not to come all day."

I shiver whenever his digits pass over my urethral opening. It seems I have so many more nerve endings there today.

"Very hard, Sir. But I did it. For you. I want to come so badly for you right now."

"I know you do, but coming is for good girls."

"I've been good!"

"You disobeyed me."

"I didn't!"

He stops fondling me. No...

"Good girls don't lie," he says.

"I'm not lying."

He sinks two fingers into my slit. *Oh, Jesus, that feels good.* I could probably come in less than two minutes.

"You sure about that?" he asks.

Crap. How does he know I'm lying? Is he just testing me? If, somehow, he knows I'm lying, will he be even more upset if I don't fess up? Or will it not matter what I say from here on out because I already messed up? What should I do?

"Why do you think I'm lying, Sir?" I inquire.

"I don't think, princess. I know."

How? Is he a walking lie detector?

"But because you did do something good," he continues, "I'll let you pick how you want to be punished."

Withdrawing his fingers, he gently caresses my clit, keeping my arousal high enough that I dismiss the need to pee for now.

"Spanking," I suggest.

"We've done a lot of that, but go on."

"Flogging."

"We can do that. What else?"

"I could give your friends another round of blowjobs and suck you off good, Sir."

"How about getting your holes filled with their cocks?"

"Sure!"

I actually don't consider that a punishment. I've fantasized about gangbangs plenty of times.

He pinches my clit and tugs. I grunt. Please fuck me now. My body has never been this wound up before.

"Let's start with the sucking off bit," Jack says.

I hear a zipper. Next his hand is behind my head, pushing me forward until I feel the bars of the cage against my face.

"Can we take the hood off first, Sir?"

"No. Now open your mouth."

Feeling his cock at my lips, I take him in, swallowing as much as I can, though my being perpendicular to him makes the angle of penetration difficult. Through the hole in the hood, I try my best to blow him. It takes work, with the tip of his cock occasionally poking into my cheek. Meanwhile, he feels me up, grabbing my breasts and tugging on the nipples. I whimper against his cock.

He pulls his cock out, and though I'd happily give him head, the position wasn't easy. I hear him walking around to the other side.

"Scoot your ass back," he directs, assisting me by sliding his arm between my legs and pulling my pelvis toward him until my rump is against the cage bars.

He adjusts my body so that my legs are flush against the bars too. The cage isn't wide enough for me to stretch myself out, so I'm bent at the waist and neck, my body curled in the shape of a cane. Feeling his flesh pressing into my backside, I practically jump for joy. I want him inside me so badly. Normally, I'd voice this sentiment, but with Jack, I'm a little wary about revealing too much to him. He might use it against me.

He sinks the head of his penis in. *OMG*. It's a novel angle for me. Can't tell if I like it better or worse than other positions because I only care about the fact that he's in me. It's amazing. Hard and thick. My pussy has been dying for this for hours.

More, I silently entreat him.

And he does provide more, pushing further into me.

Oh no. I'm going to come. Should I ask permission? What if he says no? I try and resist coming. But it feels too...damn...good.

When he withdraws, I shiver. When he sinks back in, I moan. If he keeps this up, there's no holding back my climax.

Oh shit.

He barely has to move. His cock drags against my arousal, and I come undone. I try to contain my orgasm, even though I know it's fruitless to hide it from him. My body jerks, bumping me into the cage bars. My limbs tremble, and the euphoria tumbles me beneath its monster waves. After hours of deprivation, the release feels heaven-sent.

It's not my favorite orgasm, but it's the one I appreciate the most because it freed me from all the tension that had been built inside me. I wasn't even sure if I screamed. My body continues to shudder though Jack slows to a stop and pulls out. I'm given only the briefest of moments to enjoy the afterglow of coming.

"Did you just come without permission, Casey?" he asks.

Crap. I was so focused on not coming that I forgot.

Chapter Thirteen

Kai

"Use me, Sir," Casey replies as if she hasn't heard my question. "Your little slut needs to be used."

Not letting her change the subject, I say, "So that's a 'yes'."

"You said I was supposed to save my orgasm for you, Sir. I went the entire day without coming, even though I really, really wanted to. I've never wanted to come so badly in my life."

"And you just did. Without permission. That was naughty. Disrespectful. Greedy."

"I am a greedy little whore, a greedy whore that's yours to use. Make yourself come inside of me, Sir."

"Oh, I will, princess," I say as I admire her backside. I want nothing more than to fuck the daylights out of her. "I might use you twenty-four-seven, to make the most of our time together. Think you can handle that?"

"Do I have a choice?"

"Smart girl."

I partially withdraw my cock before slamming into her. She bumps into the bars in front of her. As I thrust, the cage, suspended from the ceiling and tethered to rings on the floor, creaks and sways a little. Placing a hand on her hip, I hold her in place. The heat of her pussy, the wetness, makes my head swim. Feeling myself about to boil over, I slow my pace. I want to blow my load inside her, but I have more in store.

Withdrawing completely, I walk over to a dresser and return with a zapper and an arousing serum, which I apply to her clit.

"Mmm, that tingles," she remarks.

I run my finger over her pleasure bud. "You need more training in orgasm control. No more coming without permission."

"Yes, Sir."

For several minutes, I work her up till I see her struggling not to come. I touch the zapper to her buttock. She yelps and jerks away.

"Get on your knees," I instruct.

With her ankles and wrists still bound, it's not the easiest maneuver, but she succeeds.

"Back it up towards me," I direct.

She shuffles as far as she can go. I reach through the bars for her hip to pull her ass closer till it rests on top of her heels, then I flip her skirt over her waist. Her breasts press against the top of her thighs. I untie her ankles and pull her feet apart so I have better access to pussy. After wetting my cock with her nectar, I aim it at her asshole.

"You an anal slut, princess?" I ask.

"Yes, Sir, but I don't give it away to just anyone."

I press myself in. She grunts. Since her rectum feels fairly tight, I believe her. Gathering more of her wetness, I spread it over my shaft before going back in.

"Ugh," she groans.

Knowing she likes the dirty talk, I say, "You know that only the sluttiest whores take it in the ass."

"Yes, Sir."

My head feels ready to explode as I push my cock further. The tightness. I want to bury my whole length in one shove, but she's not wet enough for me to go rough.

"God, that feels so good," she moans.

"Keep it still for me," I tell her before touching the zapper to a buttock.

With a yelp, she jumps and almost comes off my cock.

"I said to keep it still," I reprimand, pushing her back down with one hand while zapping her again.

She cries out. Her body jerks.

"If you don't keep your ass on my cock, it's going to be all zapping and no fucking," I threaten.

"I'll try, Sir."

I zap her buttock. She yelps and twitches. I rock my hips. Her ass feels fucking incredible. I touch the zapper to an exposed part of her tit.

Not expecting it there, she screams, "Fuck!"

I zap a buttock again, and her body starts to lurch forward. She manages to catch herself in time and settles back onto my cock. Her whole body, including her rectum, is tense.

"Show me how good you can fuck my cock," I say.

Standing still, I let her move up and down my shaft. I lean back a little, forcing her to smush her ass against the cage bars, before shoving forward.

"Oof!" she grunts.

I give a few good thrusts for my own benefit before pulling out. I jerk myself to the finish and unload my cum on her backside. I savor the release, feeling the remains of my climax throbbing through my veins. I have got to get more of that ass later.

After pulling up my pants, I switch the zapper for a vibrator, which I place between her legs. Within minutes, she asks to come.

I turn the vibrator off. "That wouldn't help with your training."

Her body sags. She mutters, "You mean my punishment."

I grin. "That, too. Try to get some rest. There's more training—punishment—coming your way."

I wipe down the vibrator, set it away, and turn off the lights.

"Wait!" she exclaims. "I still need to pee!"

I turn the lights back on and, seeing a bucket, I set it underneath the cage. Taking the hood off her, I show her the bucket.

She frowns. "You're kidding, right?"

"Do I look like the kidding type, princess?"

She stares at me, waiting for me to reveal it was just a joke after all.

"Good night," I say and turn to leave.

It's actually nearing dawn, but there are no windows in the basement. Making my way upstairs, I head to my bedroom on the second floor.

Fuck me, that was fun.

At first, I didn't think much about playing out Casey's fantasy, but her enthusiasm is rubbing off on me. I was into the scene so much I didn't notice I had a missed call from Andrian. I had texted him earlier that I had Casey.

"So where you now?" Andrian asks when I call him back.

"My cabin near Tahoe," I respond.

"I'm in New York. Lukashenko let me go. I had to promise him half my testicles, so this plan better work."

"We got the daughter, didn't we?"

"Was it difficult?"

"She set the trap herself, asking to be kidnapped."

"Yeah?"

"It was a sexual fantasy of hers, and I fulfilled it."

"Nice. You fuck her?"

For some reason, I hesitate. I'm not sure why it's an issue. Andrian took me to my first brothel when I was barely a teenager. We've even been in the same room having sex with our respective partners.

"Yeah," I reply. "She still thinks we're just acting out her fantasy. She has no idea the real reason I've kidnapped her. You get any more info on Callaghan?"

"Lukashenko is calling me. Let's talk later."

After the call, while I'm taking a shower, I start wondering how Casey will react when she learns the truth. Hurt? Afraid? Devastated? I shouldn't even care, but I toy with the possibility of keeping the fantasy going until the very end. She doesn't need to know. She's just a pawn.

There's nothing more I need to do with her now. She's tied up in the basement, and that's where she can stay until we make arrangements with Callaghan for the exchange. His daughter for the SVATR laptop.

Provided the man wants his daughter back. Is he the kind of father who would throw his own offspring under the proverbial bus?

Chapter Fourteen

Kai

The day starts cloudless and sunny. The sort of day that allows people to ski in shorts.

Having changed into a sleeveless tee and sweats, I head down to the basement with a glass of water for Casey. I find her lying on her side, her panties still around her knees, the cum on her body dried.

"Look at you," I say as I approach the cage. "You're a slutty mess. You get any sleep?"

"You think you can sleep in this thing?" she returns.

"No, it'd be too uncomfortable," I acknowledge. I hold up the glass of water. "Got something for you to drink."

"My hands are still tied."

I hold the glass up to the bars. She rolls onto her knees and positions her face close to the bars. I tilt the glass over her lips. Some of the water makes it into her mouth, the rest makes its way down to the concrete floor.

"Is there anything for breakfast?" she asks.

"What do you think this is? A hotel?"

She looks down. "No, Sir."

"If you're a good little sex slave, maybe you'll get bread with your water."

She looks partially intrigued, probably liking the sex slave idea. "I'll be good, Sir."

"I see you've used the bucket," I note.

"Pissing in a bucket was not part of my fantasy," she says.

"This isn't your fantasy anymore, princess. It's mine."

Her eyes widen.

"So be grateful for what you have," I continue. "It could be worse. A lot worse. Got that?"

"Yes, Sir."

"Now let's see that pussy."

She lies down with her knees up and apart. I reach through the cage and curl two digits into her. She shivers.

"Still hot and wet," I remark.

"It's been like that for you since yesterday morning."

Gently, I stroke her. "You think you could come fast for me?"

Her eyes light up. "Yes, Sir. I've been dying to come. Even if this cage was a luxe bed with a down topper, I probably would have had trouble sleeping. You left me...unfinished."

"Part of your training. And punishment."

"I did good, didn't I?"

"You didn't have a choice."

Her lips form a pout.

I run my fingers over her swelling clit before sinking back into her snatch. Her lashes flutter.

"I don't have a choice whether to come or not, either," she says.

"Because you lack the proper training."

When I withdraw my fingers, her brow furrows.

"Please let me come, Sir. I've done everything you asked."

"No you haven't. You might be able to get away with your little lies at home, but you're not in Kansas anymore, princess."

I can see the conflict written on her face. Part of her likes being tormented, likes being pushed to her limits. Part of her is worried. She's not a complete ditz. She knows she's put herself in a vulnerable position. And the spoiled part of her just wants to indulge, to have her dessert without having to work for it.

Knowing that she must feel cramped, I decide to let her out of the cage. I scoop her up and set her on the floor. "Now what would a good little sex slave do to make her master happy?"

"Suck you off and have you come all over my face," she answers.

"We could start with that."

I pull my pants down and stroke my cock to hardness while she gets up on her knees. She takes me into her mouth and goes to work.

"Nice," I compliment when she swallows all of me without choking.

I let her do all the work until she begins to tire. Then I fixed my hand into her hair to keep the motion going.

There's no better way to start the morning than with a blowjob. My balls boil with arousal. When I start thrusting my hips, she starts to gag, but it feels too good to stop.

"Look at me when I'm fucking your face," I bark.

As she gazes up at me, her makeup smudged around her eyes, she reminds me of Athena. Trusting, eager to please.

Not liking the perk of guilt I shove it down by forcing my cock deeper and harder into Casey. She gags again.

"Keep those eyes on me," I growl, yanking on her hair for emphasis.

She snaps her gaze back at me.

She's just a pawn, I remind myself. The daughter of a man who dared to wrong me. A submissive who wants to be used and abused by me. I'm just giving her what she wants.

With a forceful grunt, I shove into my climax. I pull out so I can shoot my come into her face. My junk lands on her eyelid, her cheek, and her lips.

Licking some of it off, she grins. "Yum. Creampie for breakfast."

I can't resist a chuckle. With my thumb, I wipe a glob dripping over her eye and put it in her mouth. She sucks my thumb hard. As if she can make yourself come by doing that.

"That's enough," I say, pulling on my pants. I go back to the dresser and return with a pair of medical scissors I use to cut away bondage tape or rope in emergencies.

"Sex slaves don't deserve clothes," I explain before cutting away her sweater, top and skirt. Before cutting away all her clothes. Next, I take off her boots. Now the only thing she's wearing is my cum and those of my men.

"Ow!" She exclaims when I pull her to her feet by her hair.

Scooping her up, I lay her on top of the closed cage. Turning her on her side, I undo the binding at her wrists.

She sighs in relief. "Thank you, Sir."

I retie her wrists to the bars, one on each side of the cage. Bending each leg back, I tie her ankles to the cage bars. Standing between her spread knees, I admire her waxing job. With my thumb, I toy with her clit.

She makes little noises and eventually asks, "Do I get to come, sir?"

"A little soon, princess," I answer as I spread her wetness around the glistening nub. "Let's see how big this bud can get."

From the dresser, I bring over a suction machine. I set it by her side, lubricate the edge of the tubes, and attach one to her clit. The machine does its work, pulling her nub of flesh into the tube.

"Do you want to try the nipples, too?" I ask, even though I've already decided.

"Yes, Sir," she says, still enthralled with how large her clit can get.

After applying the suction to her nipples, I leave the tubes attached and go back to the dresser for the clothespins and string. She lifts her head and watches as I pinch the side of her breast, lay the string on top, and secure it all with a clothespin. An inch or two down, I use another clothespin, then another. Every now and then, I glance at her to gauge her reaction as I make a trail of clothespins down one side of her breast, torso and pelvis. I repeat the trail on her other side, making a nice zipper with the clothespins.

"Two more," I say of the remaining clothespins. "Stick out your tongue."

At first she balks, but she knows better than to disobey me. When she sticks out her tongue, I attach the clothespins, then step back to admire how she looks with clothespins and tubes protruding from her. My cock starts to harden. I get a flogger and flick it on the exposed parts of her body. She winces as I snap the tails more sharply. Flogging harder, I knock two of the clothespins off. She grunts loudly. Whipping the flogger at her crotch, I loosen the seal of the tube on her clit. It falls off.

"You should see how swollen your clit is," I say, fondling the engorged bud.

She immediately whimpers and strains against her bonds. I bet she could come in minutes.

"You wouldn't dare come until we're done with your punishment, would you," I warn.

She stares up at the ceiling, possibly trying to imagine away my touch. I help her out by ceasing my strokes.

I detach the tubes form her nipples. "And these must be extremely sensitive, too."

She squirms when I roll one of her enlarged nipples between my thumb and forefinger. A gentle tug produces a squeal from her, followed by what sounds like cursing when I take the nipple into my mouth and start to suck.

"Oh my God," she seems to say with the clothespins preventing her from closing her lips.

I swirl my tongue over her nipple, nibble on it, and suck some more. At the same time, I reach my hand between her legs and caress her.

"Oh, no," she moans. "P-ease..."

I move to the other nipple while curling my fingers into her cunt. Her grunting and writhing heats up my groin. Knowing there's no way she can hold back her climax for much longer, I stop.

Straightening, I pick up the end of one of the strings and yank the clothespins off one side of her body. Her scream reverberates off the concrete walls. I rub her clit while she pants.

Picking up the end of the other string, I say, "I can rip the clothespins off slow, or I can do it fast. Because you've been good so far, I'll let you choose."

"Hasss," she answers.

"Are you trying to say 'fast?'"

She nods.

"Okay. On the count of three. One...two..."

The clothespins go flying. She wails in agony, her body straining to one side. I let her gasp and settle back down before removing the clothespins off her tongue.

She stares at me. "You did that on purpose."

I grab her face, my fingers digging into her cheeks. "You accusing me of something, princess?"

Chapter Fifteen

Casey

His gaze locks with mine. I know the proper submissive would back down, lower her eyes, and apologize. But, despite all that I've been through, or possibly because of it, the rebel in me doesn't want to. Of course I'm afraid of the consequences, but I've survived everything he's thrown at me so far. The only thing I really dread at the moment is being left alone in the cage again, without having come. God, I want to come so badly. I've never been this turned on before. My body is crackling with sensitivity, each nerve throbbing with aliveness. I'm a firecracker about to explode.

"Yes," I dare. "You're a sadistic motherfucker, and I love it."

My answer seems to amuse him. "Of course you do."

"We're a good fit, you and I."

He releases me. "We'll see about that."

I watch him get what I think is called an Eroscillator and hold it to my clit. Oh no. I'm in trouble. He turns it on, and I nearly jump out of my skin.

Shit! I'm going to come in seconds!

But he takes it off my clit. I feel the nub pulsing, so close to the finish line. I draw in several long breaths. He hasn't given me permission to come yet.

"Sir, may I—"

"No."

Asshole.

"Please," I beg. "I need to come so badly."

He gives me a sympathetic smile. "I know you do."

He resumes the vibrations against my clit, but only for a few seconds. My pussy throbs with need.

"Please, please, please," I say. "I'll do anything you want!"

"Of course you will. You don't really have a choice."

I let his words sink in. What does he mean by that? Is he suggesting he's not going to honor the safeword?

"I could have my friends come down and fuck you to pieces," he explains. "Host a party and put you on display, let all the attendees feel you up, inspect your holes, and cover you with cum. Maybe I'll sell you to the highest bidder."

He stares at me with a graveness I don't expect, like he actually means what he says as opposed to painting a scenario to arouse me.

"Would you like that, princess?"

Not sure if he's being serious, I reply, "Maybe."

"You know there's nothing to stop me from selling you into the sex trade. Pretty thing like you with a taste for kink could net some good change."

He's joking. He's too rich to need to do anything like that.

When I look away in thought, he grabs my jaw to turn me back to him. "Or I could keep you for myself. Make you a bona fide sex slave. Trust me, it's not as much fun when it's not a fantasy. This shit actually happens in real life."

Okay, now he's beginning to creep me out a little. His statements remind me that Chase is probably sitting in his car, wishing I'd hurry up and let him know when we can get back home. I should probably text him an update in case he's worried. For the first time ever, I'm kind of glad my dad has a bodyguard on me. If it weren't for Chase, and what Jack describes is real, then I'd be in serious trouble. Bound to a cage, naked, I'm completely at Jack's mercy.

As if he can see my realization, Jack lets go of me and looks satisfied. He places the vibrator back at my clit. "What have you learned?"

Learned? I don't get it. Did he say what he did to arouse me or freak me out? Why would he be trying to teach me anything?

Turning off the vibrator, he slaps me a few times. "Answer the question."

"Not to trust assholes," I reply.

"And how do you know if a guy is an asshole? Did you know I was one?"

I stare deep into his eyes. They're so dark, and he's so hard to read. "Are you one?"

"Yes, I am."

A shiver runs up my spine. My pulse has quickened. "Sooo, all that stuff you just said, you mean it? You'd sell me to someone?"

He doesn't answer right away, which makes me more nervous.

"You're not ready," he replies. "You have a lot more training to go through."

He's kidding. He's got to be kidding.

He turns on the vibrator and runs it up and down my clit. Though my arousal took a dip, it quickly returns. With his other hand, he massages a breast. I *love* having his warm, strong hands on my body. Some men might as well have paws for hands, but all of Jack's grips, all his caresses, feel spot-on. And even though I wouldn't actually want to go through any of what he described, the fantasy of it turns me on, especially the one about being his sex slave.

"Please, Sir, can I come?" I ask as politely as I can. "I'll take care of that hard-on for you really good."

But a knock on the door interrupts us.

A voice says through the door. "Andrian's trying to reach you."

"Give me a minute," Jack responds, turning off the vibrator.

Dammit!

He unties my bonds, which isn't as great as coming, but I'm glad not to be tied to the cage anymore. He throws me over his shoulder, opens the cage, and puts me back in.

"Wait!" I protest as he closes the top and locks it in place.

"You're going to save that orgasm for later," he tells me. "No coming while I'm gone. I'll be watching."

I grab the bars. "You're coming right back, right?"

He gives me an amused look before walking up the stairs and out the door.

Frustrated, I kick at the cage. Of course that doesn't help. At least he left the light on so I'm not in complete darkness.

What does he mean he's watching? Does he have a spycam on me? I look around and actually spot a camera in one corner of the ceiling. Maybe if I faced the other way, he would only see my back and not know for sure if I was playing with myself? I turn around and notice another camera. Why does he have cameras in the basement to begin with? There's nothing here besides the cage I'm in, a dresser, an armoire with glass doors, a wooden pony, a St. Andrew's cross, chair and table, and a metal bed near the corner. The cameras must serve a kinky purpose.

Since I can't sit up without having to duck my head, I decide to lay down with my knees in the air. I hope he comes back really soon. Though even if he does, there's no guarantee he's going to let me come. Jack is the hardest Dom I've ever come across.

And there's more! He said something about a lot more training to go. He said that, about me not being ready, instead of what should have been the simple response to my question asking if he'd sell me: no.

He's got to be messing with my head. Doing some kind of mindfuckery. Taking this fantasy roleplaying to the extreme.

My body still hums with arousal. I wish I could will myself to an orgasm. I've had wet dreams, so it's probably possible for me to daydream myself into an orgasm. Closing my eyes, I focus on the area between my legs. I flex my pussy. I want so badly to reach down and rub myself. A few strokes on the clit. That's all I need.

But after several minutes, I don't feel anywhere nearer to a climax. What if Jack doesn't come back for hours? I wouldn't put it past him to do something like that. I don't want to be aroused for hours on end again. Maybe I should focus on cooling down instead.

After what feels like an hour, I hear footsteps. Several. Two men I don't recognize come down the stairs. I'm guessing they're two of Jack's friends. One of them is tall and black, the other of mixed race has a crooked nose and a scar across his cheek. The one with the scar gives me a lascivious grin as they just stand there, looking at me. It's a good thing I'm not shy. I haven't taken selfies of myself naked or barely dressed and posted them on a social media platform, or anything like that, but I wouldn't be opposed to doing it.

Would Jack really let his friends fuck me? Would I want to? Now that I've seen their faces, it feels more personal, so maybe no.

A few minutes later, Jack comes down.

"You did good, princess," he says. "I could tell you wanted to touch yourself."

"I did," I say. "You really know how to work me up. I'm gonna come so hard for you."

Through the bars, he taps me playfully on the nose. "If I let you."

I don't want to break the fantasy, but part of me wants to ask for my phone.

He turns to his friends. "Take her out."

After opening the cage, they grab my arms and lift me out. They set me on my feet while Jack holds a fancy-looking leather hood with an opening for the mouth.

"We're going to play a game," he says. "How much of a slut are you?"

What could I be in for? I'm both intrigued and nervous.

"Will you come on any guy's cock?" he asks.

Part of me wants to object. Liking sex doesn't make me a slut. Or if it does, I'm okay with being one. Coming on a dildo wouldn't make me a slut. What does it matter if the dildo happens to be real and attached to someone?

But being called a slut in this case is part of the fantasy. It's naughty and dirty.

"Keep your mouth open at all times," he instructs as he places the hood over my head and laces it up.

Padded on the inside at both the eyes and ears, the hood deprives me of sight and hearing. Remembering his instructions, I part my lips. Something rubbery slides through the opening and over my tongue, filling my mouth. It's a dildo. I feel it secured at the back of my head. With this thing in my mouth, how am I supposed to say my safeword?

The guys holding my arms lift me and carry me several feet forward. I'm pushed down to my knees, which land on what I think must be the mattress. Next, someone nudges my knees apart. My wrists are pulled between my thighs. I fall onto my shoulders. Cuffs are attached to my ankles and wrists. I can't move them. It might be a spreader bar locking them in place.

For several minutes, nothing happens. It's somewhat torturous. Being deprived of sight is one thing. I've been blindfolded several times before. Adding hearing is new and compounds the deprivation. It's really weird not hearing anything when I expect to hear the rustle of clothing or a guy breathing.

When a hand lands on my backside, I jump. Fingers dig into my ass, followed by a spank. Who was that?

The tall guy? I feel one hand rubbing me between the thighs, then another. The sensation reignites how much I had wanted to come before. Does this game mean I have permission to come? Jack didn't say I couldn't, though I'm always supposed to ask permission. Will there be consequences if I come? Damn this dildo in my mouth!

Holy shit! I did not expect a vibrator against my clit! This isn't fair. Of course I'm going to come, regardless of who's fucking me. Deciding I might as well make the most of this, I give in to the awesomeness of the vibrations.

Ahhh, so good...

Too soon, the vibrator is taken away. The mattress sinks a little beneath more weight. Something presses against my slit and slides inside me. The velvet hardness has to be a cock. I feel hands at my hips. Someone's pelvis slaps into my ass. Does this feel like Jack? It kind of does, but I never focused on exactly how his cock feels compared to others that I've had. Is this one a little thicker? Is the motion different?

The cock withdraws. The mattress rises as if someone has gotten up. It sinks back down. I take it someone new has taken a position behind me. This guy slams into me without ceremony and pistons away like crazy. It's more jarring than pleasurable. Maybe if he were hitting the right spot, it'd be different.

After a while, he withdraws. Something wet coats my buttock. They're all going to take a turn, I realize. I'm getting used by three different guys. Nothing like this has ever happened to me before. I never thought a fantasy like this could come true. And while I don't know Jack's friends, and the guy with the scar is kind of ugly, it doesn't matter. It's exciting and erotic as fuck.

The final cock enters me. I'm going to come on this one, whoever it is. I couldn't hold back if my life depended on it. The sensory deprivation of sight and sound enhances my other senses, and not just touch. I'm aware of the taste of the dildo. I can smell the sex filling the space, the bodies, my own arousal. My pussy clenches down on the hardness inside me, and I come undone. Finally! Bathing in euphoria, I practically cry with joy.

He—whoever he is—pulls out of me. Warm liquid lands on the small of my back.

That was so good. So. Good.

Something new pushes against my slit. Another cock? Jack did have more than two friends, I thought.

No, this feels different. It feels...round.

I squeal when it starts to vibrate inside me. This feels good, too. My pussy still throbs from the climax I just had, and now it's being stimulated again. Something colder and wet fills my asshole. Lube, I'm guessing. Oh, yes. I'm going to be filled in both holes.

Sure enough, what feels like a cock prods my backdoor, then stretches it, forcing itself into a cavity unaccustomed to receiving. I will myself to relax. The thickness continues further into me. Between the vibrations in my pussy and the fullness in my ass, I am in seventh heaven. My world has collapsed into the area below my waist. Even the discomfort of the dildo in my mouth has disappeared in favor of the intense sensations between my legs. Nothing else exists.

Gradually, the cock slides out. I let out a shaky moan, then grunt when it pushes back in. I'm going to come again, and it's going to be an even bigger orgasm this time. I curl my fingers into my palms and brace myself for the explosion, silently screaming onto the dildo when it finally rips me apart. My body feels like it wants to stretch and contract at the same time. When I finally find my voice, I curse and cry while violent tremors jerk my body in different directions.

Liquid heat fills my ass, but the vibrations continue. I can't escape them, even though my body, overwhelmed, wants a reprieve from stimulation. I'm on a plateau I can't get down from.

I feel the cock withdraw and expect the vibrating egg inside me will go next. Instead, I get a second vibrating thing at my clit. My body doesn't know what to do. Should I try and come a third time? Will that be too much? Will it even feel good?

The dildo comes in handy as I bite down on it and pray the third orgasm won't give me a stroke.

Chapter Sixteen

Kai

Casey has come twice already. The vibrator at her clit will make it three. Her toes are curled. Her hands are balled into fists. I imagine her eyes are clenched shut. I nestle the vibrator deeper into her flesh. Convulsions overcome her body. She looks like she's trying to go in all directions at once, so I hold her in place while jamming the vibrator against her. She tries to jerk away from it. I hear her babbling and sobbing. Satisfied that I've sufficiently milked her orgasm, I lower the vibrations until it's finally off. Her body continues to quiver.

Setting aside the vibrator, I remove the egg from inside her. Undoing the cuffs from her ankles and wrists, I remove the spreader bar. She collapses onto her side. Her chest continues to heave in large breaths.

I unbuckle the inward facing dildo, then unlace the hood. Her eyes seem to sparkle in the dim light of the basement as she stares at me.

"Fucking amazing," she murmurs, smiling.

With a grin, I lay down next to her and pull her into my arms. Antonne and Jay had already left, so it's just the two of us.

You were fucking amazing, I almost tell her. *And I'm not talking just your ass.*

Her ass was incredible, though. Most are. But hers felt extra special. Probably because she went through so much and came through with a smile at the end. I almost can't believe my luck. Not only do I have a bargaining chip with Callaghan, I'm having great sex.

She looks so vulnerable lying here, yet she withstood everything I threw at her so far. I'm excited for what else I can do.

Noticing her even breathing, I realize she's fallen asleep. Poor thing must be exhausted. I put her through a lot.

Without thinking, I kiss the top of her head.

She doesn't stir.

This is messed up. I should have just kidnapped her the "normal" way. Instead, I concocted this elaborate plan to execute her fantasy. I had fun. But it's crazy that she still thinks we're just roleplaying and has no clue of the potential danger she's in. If she's lucky, she'll be back with her dad in a few days. Though a remote possibility, we might not even need her.

Andrian had called to tell me he might have a lead on one of Callaghan's security detail. He sent in Dmitri to try and work the guy. If the lead proves useful, I can simply release Casey.

The thought makes me tighten my arm around her. I doze a little while she sleeps, remaining as still as I can so as not to disturb her. She'll be hungry when she wakes.

She sleeps for almost two hours.

"Don't make me pee in the bucket again," she murmurs.

"You need to go?" I ask.

She snuggles closer. "Yeah, but this is nice, too."

It's not supposed to be, but it is.

"Know who's cock you came on?" I inquire.

"Yours."

"And Antonne's."

She looks up at me, trying to figure out how or when.

I explain the progression. "It was Antonne, Jay, Antonne, then me."

"Does it really matters who's cock I came on? What did you expect when you work me up like that? You think *you* could hold back no matter who was blowing you?"

"Fair enough."

"There's such a double standard when it comes to sex. Men want women to be all horny for them, but when we actually are, we're sluts and whores. I mean, it's fun to be called one in the right circumstances, but it's not fair that the terms don't get applied to men as much."

"What are the right circumstances?"

She shrugs, then answers, "When I want to be called one. When there's no real judgment underneath, and it's just for fun."

"How can you tell if there's judgment or not?"

"You trying to be my professor or something? Hey, that would be a fun roleplay! I could be the bad student you caught cheating on her test."

I shake my head. She can have a one-track mind. I get the sense she can be like the proverbial bulldog on a bone when she really wants something.

"You're hungry," I note upon hearing her stomach growl.

"Yeah, but you know what I would really like right now? A shower. I've got crazy amounts of cum caked on me."

I help her up and let her have my shirt to wear as I show her upstairs.

"This is a beautiful cabin," she says as we pass by a room with floor to ceiling windows in which the ceiling is over twenty feet high. She spots snow outside and stops. "Where are we?"

"North Lake Tahoe," I answer.

"No way! Why are we all the way here?"

Because I didn't want any chance we'd be tracked to my house, and because this cabin is nice and secluded.

"Change of scenery," I reply casually.

"Are we near a ski resort?"

"Near enough."

She bites her bottom lip. I can tell what she wants. The temptation is too close for her not to consider it.

I lead her to my bedroom on the second floor. "You can shower in that bathroom. There's a robe on the back of the door you can use."

She opens her mouth but hesitates.

"You want to hit the slopes, don't you?" I ask for her.

Her eyes become luminescent. I don't think that word has ever really crossed my mind before.

"Go shower," I tell her.

After she closes the door of the bathroom behind her, I find Andy, who arrived earlier today, and tell him I want lift tickets, ski wear for both Casey and myself, and some regular clothes for Casey.

"Casey?" Andy echoes, clearly surprised. "You're taking her skiing?"

"Snowboarding, and why not?" I return, even though I realize it's crazy to take my kidnappee out in public. But she doesn't know she's actually my captive.

"Wouldn't 'why' be the better question?" Andy challenges.

"Because I said so."

I know what Andy is getting at, but I don't want to think too hard about the implications of one little trip to the slopes with Casey.

When she's done with the shower, we have an early dinner in the dining room overlooking the forest of pine and fir trees and the Sierra mountains in the background.

"I was thinking I should check my phone," she tells me as she digs into her lobster bisque.

I feign ignorance. "You brought a phone?"

"It was in my purse."

"I'll check with my guys, but I didn't notice a purse."

"I forgot I was supposed to check in with a friend."

"Well, if we don't find your phone, you can always use mine."

That satisfies her.

"Where'd all your friends go?" she asks.

"Doing their own thing."

"Are they skiing?"

I know for a fact they aren't, but I shrug.

"What's the nearest resort?"

"Given that it's late in the day, our options for night skiing are Boreal or Palisades Tahoe," I reply.

She does a double-take before lighting up the way I expected, the way I hoped, she would. Her jaw drops. "Are you series? Are we...? Shit! Of course I don't have my gear and ski clothes."

"It's being arranged."

She nearly knocks over her soup. "No way! Omigod!"

"You haven't been a perfect sub, but you've been good enough."

"I'm going to be the best sub you've ever had!"

She has a ways to go to earn that reputation as I've been with many experienced submissives, but it doesn't bother me that she requires more training. I wouldn't mind doing it, either. She has great potential.

She eats a good amount for dinner. Andy returns from shopping with snow pants, gloves, eyewear, knit beanies, jeans, sweaters, and more.

"You buy the whole store?" I ask of all the bags.

"You didn't give me her size, boss," he explains, "so I bought both small and medium stuff."

Andy makes a quick exist while Casey examines the clothes, picking up a pair of cute overalls with a bib. "Your friend has awesome taste! Or does he work for you?"

"Andy works for me," I acknowledge.

"That's cool that you can get him to go shopping for you. Is that what he normally does for you?"

"He's a jack of all trades."

After we've changed into our ski clothes, we take the car Andy drove up in to the rental shop for boots and boards.

"You didn't want to be closer to the slopes?" she inquires when we're driving.

I didn't get this cabin to ski. It's a place to conduct business that's somewhat remote but not too far from the Bay Area.

"I'm open to getting a place closer," I say.

"I've been itching to go snowboarding since the beginning of winter break. It's all I wanted for my birthday." She turns to me. "Out of all my friends and family, you're the only one who actually gave me a birthday gift I wanted. Thanks."

"We happen to be in the mountains, so why not?"

Truth is, there are other houses I own that I could have taken her to. But I chose Tahoe partly because she had said she loved to snowboard.

"This is my first time in this part of Tahoe," she says. "I've only been to the Southern part, near the casinos."

I can see her excitement growing as she sees the Olympic flame.

"What's the vertical drop here?" she asks.

"Twenty eight hundred, I think," I reply.

"Fucking awesome! My last ski trip was to Bitterwsweet in Michigan. It's like three or four hundred feet only."

"We'll take it slow since you haven't had that much time to acclimate."

Lake Tahoe's altitude is already over six thousand feet. The summit at Palisades Tahoe is about nine thousand feet.

After she gets outfitted for her boots and chooses her board, we hit the slopes.

Standing at the base and surveying the snow covered mountain, she sighs. "It's gorgeous. I bet the view from the upper lifts are incredible."

"They are. Depending on how you're feeling, we can go up to High Camp later."

"Yes! So what should we start with? The Kt-22 looks cool?"

"That's a black diamond run. We just got here early this morning, you haven't had a good night sleep—"

She pouts. "You sound like a parent."

"Did you forget who your daddy is?"

"Sorry, Sir."

"We'll do the Exhibition. It's part green, part blue."

"Green?!"

"Keep it up, and the only slopes you'll get are the bunny hills."

At that she buttons her lips. After the second time through the run, however, I can see why Casey wasn't ecstatic initially. She cut through the snow fairly easily and seemed to delight in going ahead of me. We try a more challenging run next. She's in her element, taking the steeper drops without hesitation. Although I'm decent on the board, Casey is clearly better. I could let her go on the tougher runs, but with her sleep deprivation and the waning daylight, I don't want to risk her running into a tree. I tell myself it's because I wouldn't want anything happening to my bargaining chip. Nothing more.

We get in a few more runs before heading up to High Camp. There, with night falling, Casey and I can still make out the mountain tops and the thick of pine trees below.

"I've never snowboarded at night," she comments, seeing the lights on one of the few runs open late.

"Maybe if you're extra good," I find myself saying, though the truth is, I'd like to take her on that run regardless. Her face has glowed with joy the whole time we've been here. I've never been up close to such enthusiasm before. And I don't think I've ever felt it before. I've had highs—my first six-figure arms deal that I did on my own before my father retired is perhaps my most memorable—but they're usually fleeting. I move on to the next thing, looking for something bigger and better, like the AI that Callaghan currently holds.

Casey looks at me with sparkles in her eyes. "I'll be good! Like, super extra good!"

My body warms at what that could mean. Pulling her to me, I drink in the sight of her, her cheeks still flush from our last run. It's crowded at High Camp, but the people around us might as well be miles away. The space between Casey and me is our own. My gaze hones in on her lips. I realize I don't know what they taste like, what they feel like. This is a part of her I haven't claimed yet.

But I'm about to.

Anticipating the kiss, she tilts her head up as I lower mine. But the buzzing of my phone pulls me away. I want to ignore it, but I needed it. Kissing Casey in some romantic backdrop is not part of the plan. Hell. Taking her snowboarding wasn't either. I'm losing my focus. I didn't expect Casey to be so...tempting. Her enthusiasm, so unadulterated and child-like, is contagious, and I wanted some of it.

She looks disappointed when I pull away to pull out my phone. It's a text from Andrian. He's on his way.

Chapter Seventeen

Casey

"You hungry?" Jack asks me after putting away his phone.

"Starving," I reply, but what I really want is to get back to the moment right before he got a text. He was about to kiss me. I know it. And we haven't kissed yet. We've had plenty of sex, sure, and it's not like I've missed kissing. Until now. Almost like in that old rom-com, *Pretty Woman*. I mean, I don't think that kissing should only be reserved for people in love, but I want to be kissed by Jake.

He looks around at the crowd of people. "How about someplace a little more quiet if you're not itching to get out of your snow gear? There's a bar outside Truckee, sort of where only locals go."

"Quiet sounds good," I say. "And I don't care about walking around in snow pants."

On the drive over, Jake's fairly quiet. Not that he's ever been much of a talker, but he seems lost in his thoughts. I probably should take the time to do my own reflecting, maybe try and figure out what might have happened to Chase. If he lost me, is he going to go to my dad and tell him everything? I can imagine my dad popping a vein in anger. He'll probably be most upset that I wasn't with Kenton.

Not wanting to dwell on my dad's potential reaction, I try to draw out Jack. "So, what do I have to do to be extra good?"

"What do you think?" he returns.

"Well, what do you mean by 'good?' A good girl or a good sub?"

"You capable of being a good girl?"

"Did I already tell you I signed up to volunteer?"

He looks at me, possibly skeptical, though I don't see what's so hard to believe.

"Yeah, for this nonprofit group that teaches kids from disadvantaged backgrounds how to ski," I explain. "Of course, I'd teach snowboarding."

He doesn't respond right away, so I find myself prattling on. "I know it's not like saving lives or anything, but a lot of kids don't have the opportunity to try a winter sport. Usually, winter sports are not like soccer or football where all you need is a field and a ball. It can be expensive for a lot of people, especially something like skiing where you have to rent equipment and buy lift tickets."

"You figure that all out yourself?"

I blush. "I read about it."

"Fields aren't necessarily easy to come by, especially in inner cities, but skiing is definitely less accessible. You actually going to go through with this volunteering?"

"I'm offended. You think I'm that spoiled that I can't handle a little volunteer work?"

He looks me in the eyes. "Yes."

The bluntness of his answer stuns me. He really thinks that? I guess I haven't given him any reason to think otherwise. If he thinks that about me, why is he spending time with me? Maybe it's just all about the sex for him, so my character flaws don't matter. It was all about the sex for me, too, except that changed at some point. In the span of a few days, he's given me the best birthday gift ever: he made a sexual fantasy come true and he took me snowboarding. He's like fucking Santa Clause.

"What do you do to be good?" I ask. "Besides rescuing alley cats?"

Looking ahead at the road, he makes a wry grin, to himself it seems. "Philanthropy."

"Yeah? Like what kind of philanthropy?"

"Supporting foster youth programs. Too many kids fall through the cracks."

"Were you one of them?"

"I was one of the lucky ones, and there aren't a lot of lucky ones."

"In what way were you lucky?"

"I was adopted by parents who treated me well. My dad was a hard ass, but that's how I knew he cared about me. I no longer had to wonder where my next meal might come from."

I think about all the things I have that he might not have had growing up. "I guess I was born super lucky then."

"You were."

"Except for the dad part. I'm not sure mine really cares all that much about me. He cares about appearances, that's for sure. That's probably why he goes to church. And to repent for his sins. I think repenting makes him feel like he can continue sinning. As long as he repents, all's good. It's such a joke."

Jack's face seems to darken. "You don't think your dad cares about you?"

"Not about my happiness, that's for sure. If he cared, he wouldn't push me to marry someone I have zero interest in marrying. I don't know that I ever want to marry."

"No Prince Charming for the princess?"

I shrug. "Don't see the point really. I mean, maybe it works for people who come from normal, healthy families. I think the only reason my parents are still married is because the Catholic church doesn't approve of divorce, though that doesn't stop my father from committing other wrongs, like adultery. He's such a hypocrite."

"You don't sound like a fan of your old man."

"'Cause he won't let me live my own life. In this country, in this day and age, he wants to choose who I'm going to marry? How backwards is that?"

"You're twenty-years old, Casey. What's stopping you from living your life?"

I don't have an answer to that question. I'm also stunned he said my name instead of calling me 'princess.' It feels like progress.

Jack continues, "How much longer are you going to live under daddy's roof while rebelling against him in passive aggressive ways?"

I raise my eyebrows. I'm beginning to see why this guy doesn't have a girlfriend. Or maybe he does and he simply hasn't told me.

But he's right, though I don't want to admit it. Except for the whole marrying Kenton thing, I haven't resisted my father on anything. Aside from the usual teenage stuff, like breaking curfew or smoking, I've been a damn good daughter, and still my father doesn't seem to see me.

I change the subject. "What about you? You plan to get married someday? Or are you cheating on your wife right now?"

He pulls up in a half empty parking lot before a dumpy looking wood structure. Not the sort of spot you expect someone with a Bugatti to patronize. I thought we were going to eat at one of the fancier places at the ski resort.

"Marriage isn't on my bucket list, either," Jack replies.

"Why not?" I ask.

"In my line of work, it's better...I'm too busy to get married."

"No one's that busy. That's just an excuse. You just don't want it bad enough."

He looks surprised and amused. "You calling me out, princess?"

"Hey, I'm not judging you. I just said I don't believe in marriage, so you're in good company."

We get out of the car and walk into the bar. It doesn't look any better on the inside, but maybe, like the Chinese noodle place Jack took me to, the quality is in the food rather than the ambiance. Unlike High Camp, I can count the number of patrons besides me and Jack on one hand. Country music plays in the background.

"It's crazy how many places in California have gluten free and vegan options," I remark upon studying the menu. "Even in a place like this."

After I order a cheeseburger and fries—with gluten and dairy—we play some darts while waiting for our food.

"You major in darts at Notre Dame?" Jack asks me after I manage to hit the bullseye twice out of six throws.

"This is maybe my third time playing," I reply.

He raises his brows. "Back up and try it again."

I take several steps back. The first one I throw hits the outer bullseye. The second hits the double ring.

"You've played more than three times," he says when I nearly hit another bullseye after four more throws.

"Honest, I haven't," I say. "Maybe it's beginner's luck."

"That or you have incredible hand-eye coordination."

I look at him mischievously. "I'll play you for something."

He leans back against a pool table and crosses his arms. "You think I'm stupid or blind?"

"We can make it challenging. If I hit the bullseye, which is hardly a guarantee, we stay another night here and you take me snowboarding again tomorrow."

"And if you miss?"

I give him a sultry smile. "What do you want?"

"If you miss, we stay another night and you give up your safe word."

My heart stops. Given what Jack's capable of, that's fucking scary. I like it. Adrenaline tingles through me.

But I know it's not wise. Can I trust him? So far, he's looked out for me. He's been protective even, not letting me snowboard the harder runs right away. But what if he overestimates what I can handle?

Damn. I've never been in a lot of predicaments before. Like Jack alluded to, I've lived a fairly charmed life. I shouldn't have gotten so cocky about the dark throwing, but I didn't think he'd come back with the safe word shit. I thought maybe he'd want a dozen blow jobs or something. Next time, I'll think things through a little more.

"How many shots do I get?" I ask.

"One."

"One chance to make a bullseye? That's crazy. I'm not that good."

"Bullseye or inner ring," he offers.

Now my heart picks up speed. Returning to where I stood before, I look at the dart board. It's doable. I could get lucky, too. And I don't want to back out since I was the one who proposed the game in the first place.

Dart in hand, I take a deep breath and aim.

Chapter Eighteen

Kai

"Mind if I use your phone again?" Casey asks me on the drive back to the cabin.

I hand it over to her. She dials the number for her bodyguard, and it goes straight to voicemail. She furrows her brow.

"I'm gonna text my dad, let him know I'm with a, um, friend," she says.

At some point she's going to learn that she's my captive, in reality, not just fantasy. But I find myself wondering if it's possible to keep up the charade to the end and spare her any potential trauma from knowing the truth.

Raphael Lee, another member of the *Jing San* whom I look up to as an older brother, is strict about not letting zeros—civilians not associated with gangs or organized crime—get caught in the crosshairs of what we do. Casey isn't a zero because of her father, but she also didn't choose to be born into the mafia.

After handing back my phone, she says, "That was a fucking good burger and fries. And the guac on it was awesome."

She had scarfed the burger down like there was no tomorrow. I thought she was going to order a second one.

"Do you get to come up here whenever you want?" she asks me.

"Pretty much," I reply.

"You're so lucky."

"Pay your dues in life, and you might end up lucky, too."

She knits her brow. "Like, what kind of dues?"

"Figure it out, princess."

She pouts, probably expecting me to provide her the answer.

"What do you want out of life?" I elaborate. "And what are you willing to do or sacrifice to get it?"

She turns the question on me. "What did you want out of life?"

To be the best arms dealer in *Jing San* history, I silently reply.

"To be the best at what I do," I answer instead.

"You're not the best already?"

I will be once I get that SVATR laptop back from your fucking dad.

"Almost," I say.

"Why do you want to be the best? Seems like you're already pretty successful. It's not like you need more money, right? Unless you want to build a rocket to Mars or buy up some island country."

"Honor," I tell her. "For myself. For my father, who was in the same line of business."

She looks like she's trying to wrap her head around the idea, eventually responding with, "Cool."

"So what are you after in life?" I inquire. It's not a question I should be asking. She's my captive, my hostage. What does it matter what she wants?

"A good time."

No surprise there. My father would have disdained such a frivolous answer. But I can see the appeal. Maybe I'll take a piece of that—after I get my laptop back and this deal done.

"But, honestly," she continues, "I'd settle for independence. I mean, I'm twenty-one years old, right? But I feel like I'm still a child because I depend on my parents."

"So don't. Your independence is there. You just have to take it."

She becomes quiet, then, as if that's enough serious talk for her, she smiles at me. "I'm also after the perfect Dom."

"No such thing as perfection when it comes to humans."

"You're pretty perfect."

I meet her glimmering gaze. "You might think differently without your safe word."

"Omigod! I was *sooo* fucking close. The big, bearded guy coughed just as I was throwing the dart. Otherwise, it would have been a bullseye."

"I believe it."

"I should have been allowed a do-over."

I pull the car up to the cabin and say without sympathy, "Life's a bitch."

She purses her lips. "You're not very nice."

I grab her by the jaw and pull her to me. My stare digs into hers. "Never said I was. In case you have any doubts, I'm the bad guy, princess. And I don't transform into a prince at any point in time."

So you should run. Run far away from me.

Her lashes flutter, and for a few seconds, she seems to absorb my warning. But then that fearless, reckless part of her emerges.

"What if I fucked you really hard?" she asks as mischief radiates from her eyes.

Fuck me. I can't believe this woman. Of course, she doesn't know I was speaking in earnest, but she still surprises me.

As if I want to know the answer to her question, I yank her to me and crush my lips to hers. I can taste the salt from her fries. And then there's her. The taste of her, wet and warm as I dig my tongue into her mouth. I devour her with a hunger I didn't know I had. Over and over, I consume her, barely cognizant of how the bruising force might be too much for her. The kiss isn't just about giving in to passion; it's a warning, echoing my earlier words.

But she's not backing down. She's not succumbing. She gives it back with her own fervor. And that makes the heat flare throughout me.

We're still in our ski clothes, and I doubt Andy would be ecstatic to have us fuck in his car. But I don't want to wait.

Without parting our lips, I shift the car seat back, then pull Casey over. She straddles me while I continue to ravage her mouth. Threading her fingers through my hair, she tugs hard. I didn't give her permission to do that, but I like it. Putting a hand to the back of her head, I shove her lips further into mine, taking every breath of hers. She starts to struggle for more air. I move to her neck, taking large mouthfuls while she gyrates her hips, grinding herself atop me.

After pulling down the straps of her overalls, I pull out her sweater and thrust both hands beneath. I caress her back, grasp her waist, and grope a breast through her hot pink sports bar. Her sighs and murmurs fill my ears, edging my ardor. I yank her bra above her breasts. The tight band of the bra presses the orbs down. Reaching for one, I bring the nipple to my mouth.

She gasps. "Shit, they're still sore!"

Good. I assault the hardened nub even more.

"Shit!" she swears again, squealing when I bite and suck the nipple harder.

Giving her a reprieve, I return to kissing her. She mauls me with her mouth, possibly to prevent me from going back to her nipple. She humps my leg.

Fisting my hand in her hair, I pull her head back. "You looking to come on my leg?"

"Please," she murmurs.

Feeling like I could lose myself in her, I force myself to regain control and take a breather. Releasing her hair, I grab my scarf from the backseat and bind her forearms behind her back. I can tell she wants to get back to what she was doing before, but she waits patiently as I rip out a thread from the hem of her sweater. Once it's long enough, I sever it, fold it several times to thicken the string, and wrap one end around her nipple.

She sucks in her breath. "You want to make it hurt, don't you?"

I look at her. "Don't you?"

She nods.

The other end of the string goes past her shoulder and around the handle of the rearview mirror to provide a constant tug on her nipple.

"Now do it," I command, holding her waist with my right hand so she doesn't scoot away and slacken the string. "Fuck my leg."

Slowly, she rocks her hips, rubbing her pussy along my thigh. I wonder that she can feel much through her ski pants.

"Come on," I urge. "You said you'd fuck me really hard."

She makes more of an effort but winces when her movement causes the string to pull on her nipple. I slap her other breast.

"*Hard*," I remind her.

"Yes, Sir."

At that, she grinds herself to me in earnest. I alternate between grabbing her hips and helping her and groping her other breast.

"This nipple could use a little pain," I say of the left one. Catching it between my thumb and forefinger, I twist it. She yelps. I pull it toward the window.

Her body moves in that direction, but that causes the string to pull on the other nipple more.

"Fuck me," she swears through gritted teeth.

Seeing tears in her eyes, I release the nipple. Diving my hand into her pants, I find my way into her panties to fondle her.

"God, that feels good," she murmurs. "Am I allowed to come?"

"You think I'm nice enough to let you come so soon?"

She meets my gaze. I feel an unexpected stab of guilt but bury the feeling. *She* approached *me*. She didn't have to.

"Eventually?" she asks.

"We'll see."

I push her away to unzip my pants and pull out my cock. She licks her lips while I stroke myself to full hardness.

"Let's see how hard you can fuck," I say, undoing her pants and yanking it down her legs.

She swears as the movement causes the string to pull on her nipple. Even after I recline the driver's seat, it's not easy for her to climb onto my cock, but I can see the determination in her eyes. She's tougher than I expected. Locking her gaze with mine, she sheaths herself on my cock. My eyes want to roll to the back of my head. Fuck, she feels good. So good.

In the cramped confines of the car, her arms tied behind her, a string pulling on her nipple, it won't be easy for her, but grimacing through the pain in her nipple, she slides herself up and down my length. The gliding of her hot wet flesh against mine sends my arousal boiling.

I'm impressed by her efforts, but I want more. "You're going to have go harder than that if you want to fuck the asshole out of me."

She presses her lips together and, even though she might be sore from the snowboarding, pumps her thighs like a champion. She cries out when the string breaks.

"That's it," I encourage. "Fuck me hard."

She cranks it up. Huffing and grunting, she drills herself on my cock. After all this, she deserves an orgasm.

"Make yourself come," I tell her.

I didn't think she had another gear to go to, but somehow she digs deep to go harder and faster. My balls are about to burst. I have to grab her hips and slow her or I'll blow it. Closing my eyes, I hold back the ejaculation while riding my peak. I wait for the euphoria to settle. Once the temptation to shoot my load passes, I start thrusting up into her. My turn.

She smiles at me. "You going to fuck the princess out of me, big boy?"

"That's 'Daddy' to you, princess."

"Bring it on, Daddy."

Holding her in place by the hips, I slam my pelvis into her, forcing out a loud cry. I go so hard and fast, she looks like a ragdoll being shaken by an angry child. She barely has the chance to scream or grunt. I slow to give her a reprieve. The windows of the car have completely fogged up, and we're both sweating profusely thanks to the ski apparel and our exertions. Wanting her to come, I roll my hips more tenderly and put my thumb against her clit.

"I'm gonna come," she murmurs.

A minute later, I feel her pussy fluttering against my cock. Her body spasms atop mine. Since I didn't ejaculate, I could come again, but I want to focus on her orgasm. I want to milk every drop.

When the shivers finally cease, she falls atop me, wincing when her nipple grazes me. Our breaths still heavy, I savor the feeling of still being joined to Casey, my cock thick inside her still pulsing pussy.

I stroke the back of her head. "Not bad for a princess."

"I thought my thighs were going to give out," she mutters. "And I wish I didn't have nipples."

I chuckle. We recline together in quiet until my cell buzzes with a text message. I hold Casey to me while I reach for my phone. It's Andrian. He's almost here.

Chapter Nineteen

Kai

B ack in the cabin basement, I take it easy on Casey, edging her only twice before we both come in flatiron position, first in her vagina, then in her ass. After withdrawing from her, I spoon her into my arms. My gaze takes in her nakedness as she curls upon the bed. I graze the golden down at her mound and tease her clitoris. I want to make her come again, but she also looks a little spent.

"Mmm," she purrs, her eyes still closed. "Between the snowboarding and the awesome sex, this day couldn't get any better."

Deciding not to cast doubt on her sentiment, I say, "Glad you feel that way. I've got a surprise."

"Yeah?"

"I've got another friend coming."

Opening her eyes, she frowns a little. "A female friend?"

"No. He's an old friend whom I go way back with, to my younger days when I lived at the border of China and Russia."

"So is the surprise a threesome?"

I don't know. I don't want to share Casey at the moment, but Andrian hasn't met a pretty woman he wouldn't fuck.

I ask Casey if she wants a drink. Her eyes go back to being closed while she answers in the affirmative.

Upstairs, I put on a pair of sweatpants. As I fill a glass with water, I hear the squeal of tires. Without looking out the window, I know the tires go to a bright blue Lamborghini.

Andrian is here.

"*Zdarova*!" he greets when Andy and I, holding the glass of water, step into the foyer.

Andrian stands an inch shorter, though for most of our youth he had been the taller one. He has strawberry blond hair, sunken eyes and a resting frown. Given to looking stylish, Andrian wears a button-down shirt, open at the top with a gold cross around his neck, jeans and a leather jacket. In one hand, he holds a cigarette. He almost always has a tobacco product. Behind him stands his bodyguard, Lev.

"Look sexy, my friend," Andrian says, gesturing at my bare chest. "Hey, your guy at the door made Lev show him all his weapons like you don't know us."

"Tao is new and always thorough," I explain.

Andrian turns to Lev. "The gift."

Lev presents a box.

"A rare bottle of the best Stoli," Andrian explains, "to toast our victory. Even though the drive here was shit with traffic, I am ready. We can call Callaghan tonight, yes?"

"Let's discuss first so we can give Callaghan the final details in one call and minimize the amount of time he has to cook up mischief."

I turn to give the glass of water to Andy. "Bring this down to Casey."

"I forgot she is here," Andrian remarks. "Let me see this *suka*. We can take picture of her in tears to send to fucking Callaghan."

He starts to follow Andrian to the basement, but I stop him. "You can see her after we talk."

"Why?"

"She doesn't know she's been kidnapped."

"Ah, yes, she thinks this is sex fantasy," Andrian recalls with a rare smile. Back in Russia, I never saw Andrian smile. Granted, he didn't have a lot to smile about in his youth, but he also doesn't believe in smiling. He believes the tendency for Americans to smile a lot reflects their naive and counterfeit natures.

He looks me over. "You fuck her a lot?"

"What does that matter?"

He rubs his chin. "Maybe I fuck her, too."

I had a feeling Andrian would want to.

"She's probably asleep right now," I say.

"Good. Less resistance."

An unease swirls in my groin as Andrian heads toward the stairs to the basement, but I shouldn't care who fucks Casey. I mean I *don't* care. To prove that to myself, I decide I'll let Andrian fuck her.

"I'll take the water to her," I say to Andy so he can stay behind with Lev.

Before we reach the stairs, I grab Andrian. "Just go with the fantasy. I haven't told her who we really are yet."

"Why not tell her now?"

"Because she doesn't need to know."

Andrian looks perplexed.

"It's a lot more fun this way," I try. "As soon as we tell her, she's going to dissolve into a crying, frightened woman. I don't want to fuck that."

"You should try. Is fun, too. Sometimes the more they cry, the better."

"Not for me."

Andrian shakes his head. "Be careful that America is not making you a *pizda*."

Down in the basement, Casey has fallen asleep on her side. Andrian smirks as he surveys her naked form.

"*Amerikanskaya shlyukha!*" he says, kicking the bed. "Is time Kai shared his little toy."

Looking a little groggy as she sits up, Casey looks from Andrian to me. I hand her the water and say, "You're going to be a good little sub for my friend, the way you've been with me. Got it?"

She assesses Andrian and doesn't look as eager as I would have expected, given her earlier interest in a gangbang.

I grab her chin. "Got it?"

"Yes, Sir," she replies. "I'd do anything to please you, Sir."

"*Vot eto da*," Andrian comments. "She is good slut."

He gropes one of her breasts. "Not bad for American. But Russian women prettier. Russian women most beautiful in all the world."

In my younger days, I might have agreed, but now that I've traveled the world, I've seen there are plenty of beautiful women everywhere.

Casey raises a brow at Andrian as she retreats from his grasp. "You don't have to be here. I'm sure there are plenty of Russian women in the Bay Area."

He snorts. "Eh. American pussy is better than no pussy."

"I could probably say the same about Russian cock," she retorts.

"American women love Russian dick," he corrects her.

"Since when?"

"My girlfriend says American women—what is word—simp? American women simp for Russian men. All your naughty romance books are about

Russian men. Russian men superior to American men."

"Yeah? Is that why your athletes have to cheat in order to win against ours?"

Andrian frowns. Seeing his hand ball into a fist—I know that Andrian would have no qualms hitting a woman for the purpose of violence—I step in front of him.

In Russian, I tell him, "Don't let her get to you. Let's just enjoy her."

He seems to back down but not without spitting to her, "American men are pussies. They let American women do what they want. Russian men, we know how to be tough, to be real men. That is what American women really want: real men to be in charge."

Casey turns to me. "Your friend is really evolved."

Looking to me, Andrian demands angrily, "What is she saying?"

"It doesn't matter," I reply in Russian. "You know how mouthy American women can be."

Casey eyes me. "I didn't know you speak Russian."

Andrian turns to her. "Only Americans too stupid and arrogant to speak anything but English."

"If we're so stupid, how come we're the richest country in the world? How come some of the best products come from America? Besides vodka, what's your claim to fame?"

Seeing Andrian's eyes bulge, I place myself between them again and face Casey. Her eyes widen after I slap her harder than I have before. It's for her own good. If she keeps antagonizing Andrian, she's going to get herself seriously hurt. Andrian's ego is too large—or fragile—to allow slights on his manhood or his fatherland.

"Behave yourself," I admonish her. She winces when I grab her by the hair on the top of her head. "You agreed to be a good sub. Get your act together or it gets ugly."

From the look in her eyes, I scared her more than I intended, but I need her to take notice. Releasing her hair, I take a softer tone as I caress the side of her face. "Be good, and I'll make sure we push all your buttons."

That calms and intrigues her.

Stepping back, I say to the both of them, "We going to fuck or not?"

At that, Andrian nods and rubs his crotch. "*Da,* let's fuck this *shlyukha.*"

Chapter Twenty

Kai

Andrian takes out his cock and says to Casey, "Once you have Russian dick, you will simp for more. Like all American women."

Casey only frowns as Andrian pulls and pushes his foreskin up and down his shaft.

"Should I take ass or pussy?" Andrian wonders aloud. He shoves Casey onto her stomach, then pries apart her butt cheeks to inspect her asshole. He pokes a finger into the puckered hole. "Yes, this is good. I tear it more open for you and fuck your bowels with cum."

I take in Casey's reaction. She doesn't look ecstatic, but she hasn't protested either. I toss a bottle of lube onto the bed.

Andrian dismisses it. "Is already wet."

"Doesn't hurt to use more," I reply.

"What if I want it to hurt?"

"Just use the fucking lube."

Andrian looks surprised at my tone of voice but reaches for the lube and squirts some on his cock. My body heat ticks up as I watch his tip press at her anus. She lets out a cry when he shoves himself in.

Ignoring the rise of concern within me, I tell her, "Relax, princess. You know you like getting your holes stretched by cock."

At my words, her tension decreases. Andrian thrusts deeper.

"Yes," he groans. "Take cock, you filthy whore."

Casey grunts as he pumps himself in and out of her backside. I can't tell if she's enjoying the sex.

I don't care if she is.

Nonetheless, I direct her to touch herself. She nestles her hand beneath her crotch.

"Make yourself come," I direct Casey. "Show me what a good little slut you are."

"Yes, Sir," she murmurs.

I watch as Andrian quickens his thrusting. He doesn't care if Casey is getting anything out of this.

The upside of his indifference is that he'll be done sooner. I remember the first time Andrian took me to a brothel on his side of the river. There was barely any foreplay between him and the prostitute. He wanted in and done.

Even though I have mixed feelings about Andrian fucking Casey, my own cock has turned hard.

"You look worried, Kai," Andrian says to me. "No worry. I won't break her. Yet."

At my glare, Andrian decides to be nice. "Here, you take her pussy."

He withdraws. I know he wants to remain on "top." It makes him feel like he's in charge. He thinks it makes him confident. But I see the truth in my friend and men like him. Top, bottom—it's just a position. When you're truly confident, you can command from anywhere.

Whipping off my pants, I get on the bed. Casey feels like a ragdoll when I pull her on top of me. She's tired. After we fuck her, I'll let her sleep undisturbed the rest of the night. She groans when I sheath her over my cock. Despite being thoroughly used the past forty-eight hours, she still feels amazing.

Andrian slides himself back into her ass. Now her pussy feels tighter.

"Is good, *shlyukha*?" Andrian asks her, fumbling for a breast.

She grimaces when his hand grazes the nipple that was tied to the rearview mirror in the car. He tugs on her breast. I trace her bottom lip with my thumb.

"Ready to take us both on, princess?" I ask, even though she has no choice in the matter. But I know she'll answer yes, which might help her frame of mind.

"Yes, Sir," she replies and even licks at my thumb.

I press it into her mouth. "Good."

She sucks on my thumb while Andrian releases her breast so he can focus on his thrusting. I raise my hips to provide them a better angle.

"You liking the dp?" I ask Casey.

"Yes, Sir."

I switch out my thumb for the other fingers, stretching her mouth. "Of course you do. Because you're a naughty little slut."

She gags when I press my fingers deeper. Knowing she likes the dirty talk, I continue, "A naughty slut who just wants to be used. That right?"

"Yes, Sir."

"What are you?"

She mumbles against my fingers, "A slut."

Withdrawing my digits, I fist my hand tightly in her hair, making her wince. "I can't hear you."

"A slut!"

"What kind of slut?"

"A naughty slut," she huffs. "A slut who wants to be used, who wants to be your fuck toy."

Her words make my balls boil with desire. Timing my thrust with Andrian's, I shove myself into her.

"You make a good fuck toy, princess," I tell her. It's the truth. I can't remember being aroused to these depths before. And most of it is from getting her off. "How 'bout I keep you as my fuck toy for a while? Make this basement your personal sex dungeon. Invite more guys over. See how many you can take at once. Would you like that?"

Her eyes are glossy with lust.

"Of course you would," I answer for her. "And even if you didn't want that, it doesn't matter. I can do whatever I want with you."

She seems to hear the truth in my statement and looks at me quizzically.

Andrian pumps faster, chasing his orgasm. "We send her back to Callaghan full of cum, so daddy can see his little girl is whore."

A minute later, Andrian clenches his teeth. His face becomes red. He shoves deep and almost pushes Casey off my cock. After several shudders and grunts, he withdraws and collapses onto the bed.

With my cock still hard and throbbing inside her, I let Casey lay atop me to gather herself. Some of Andrian's cum oozes out of her and drips onto my balls. A part of me wants to drill my fist into his face, a sensation I've never felt with Andrian before. While there have been plenty of times when Andrian exasperated me, I've always played the yin to his yang. I don't owe him anything because I've more than repaid him for protecting me on the streets of Blagoveshchensk when we were young, but he's my friend and also my partner in the most important sale of my career. Casey is just a spoiled young woman I barely know.

Still...

My adoptive father is big on intuition and listening to the part of the brain that only speaks in whispers. He says he owes all his successes to following his intuition and has mentioned more than once that when he met my adoptive mother for the first time, he knew they were meant to be.

It's probably just dumb luck that it worked out with the woman he felt that way about, but I do believe that our mind processes a lot more than we're cognizant of. And if I'm honest with myself, I felt a pull toward Casey the moment our eyes met. I just didn't realize it at the time because the sexual energy from the club got in the way.

Andrian's cellphone rings. Grumbling, he pulls it out and, seeing the caller, mutters in Russian, "Bitch, what the fuck?"

"Elena?" I guess.

He shakes his head. "Katya."

"Not Lukashenko's Katya," I say in Russian.

Andrian doesn't reply.

I raise a brow. "Messing with your boss' wife. That's high risk."

Quickly zipping up, Andrian turns to me. "Keep the cunt quiet."

I clasp my hand over Casey's mouth and tell her, "Don't make a sound if you want to come."

Casey remains still while Andrian, heading toward the stairs, picks up the call.

"Katya!" I hear him greet with false enthusiasm as he climbs the stairs. "I hope nothing is wrong. I only get urgent calls on my cellphone."

I release Casey only after hearing the door close.

"What was that about?" she inquires.

"His girlfriend called," I answer.

"So I take it she wouldn't approve of what he just did?"

I shrug. I don't know Katya well enough to say. I do know that Elena would have wanted to tear out Casey's eyes if she knew.

"Your friend's kind of a douche," Casey says.

"You shouldn't pick a fight with him," I warn her. "He's got a temper."

"Would he hit me or something?"

"I can't promise you he wouldn't."

My response seems to disappoint her. She raises her brows. "Would you let him?"

Disgruntled by the look she's giving me, I reply, "Didn't I tell you I'm not your knight in shining armor?"

"So you'd let him hit me? After you've already let him fuck me?"

"Who let a man she barely knew kidnap her?"

"My sexual fantasy didn't include being hit by an obnoxious Neanderthal."

"You think the world exists to fulfill your desires, princess? Stop being so naive."

Her gaze searches deep into mine, maybe looking for signs that I'm just messing with her. It's her own damn fault that she's in her current predicament. Would I let Andrian hit her? No. But I don't need to give her the impression I'm something that I'm not. Such as chivalrous. The *Jing San* is egalitarian. The opportunities as well as the consequences are the same for everyone, regardless of sex.

Casey climbs off of me. "Fuck you."

I grab her. "We're not done."

She tries to pull away. "Get your buddy to finish you off. He obviously matters more to you."

"Are you jealous?"

She starts wrestling more aggressively. "I can't believe you'd let your friend hit me. Are you not man enough to take him on—"

I throw her onto her back and pin her to the bed. "You want to say that again, princess?"

She glares at me. "Are. You. Not. Man. Enough."

I shake my head in disbelief. "I should punish you long and hard for disrespecting your Dom—and I will—but first I'm going to make you come."

At that, she tries to throw me off, but her efforts only fuel the heat between us. The wriggling of her body beneath mine is turning me on like crazy. And I know she likes being dominated.

"Don't you want to come?" I growl while she kicks.

"Not for you!"

"That's bullshit. You'll come for me wherever and whenever I say you will."

Defiance flares in her eyes.

"Cute," I comment. "Do I need to prove it to you?"

She doesn't answer right away, possibly worried that I'll do just that.

Chapter Twenty-One

Casey

His body is heavy atop mine. He's bigger and stronger. Overpowering me is a piece of cake to him. Still, I won't go down without a fight.

Problem is, I'm not entirely committed to fighting. Otherwise, I could make him pay, even if he succeeds. And he will succeed. Because my body is so goddamn attracted to him. Even though I'm pissed as hell, desire percolates in my lower body.

But we seem to have entered a more dangerous realm with the addition of his friend. Up until now, I trusted Jack. Maybe that wasn't smart of me. That's the message from Jack himself. But if he really just wanted to use and abuse me, he wouldn't have taken me snowboarding. I didn't even ask him to do that.

But I definitely don't trust this guy Andrian. His dislike of me seems genuine. Even though I challenged Jack's manhood, I don't get the sense that he's afraid of Andrian. In a physical fight, I wouldn't hesitate to bet my money on Jack, even though Andrian may be just as muscular. But Jack said he wouldn't intervene if his friend tried to hit me. I didn't expect that. It hurt. And now I'm angry. Jack isn't the man of my dreams after all.

At least he's good for a fuck. Why not let him make me orgasm one last time? Then I'll call it quits.

Looking up at him, I see a faint grin hovering over his lips. He can see I'm relenting. Even though he probably knows how much I simp for him, I resume my struggling and even try to knee him in the balls.

"Enough!" He barks. "This is piss poor sub behavior."

He slaps me across the face, then cruelly twists my most tormented nipple. I lay still.

"Good," he says, then slides himself into me. "Take your cock like a good girl."

I clench his hardness. It feels so good inside of me.

He locks gazes with me. "See that? How your pussy flutters around my cock? I own you, princess."

I want to prove him wrong and sucker punch his confidence. I want to prove it to myself as much as I want to prove it to him. I look away and try to ignore how good it feels to have him throbbing inside of me, but he flexes his cock, drawing my attention. I gasp when he adjusts his angle of penetration to a better one. When I resist, he pushes himself deeper, as if to show me that there's nowhere for me to run, there's no escape. My only hope is that he'll come before I do.

"This part of your fantasy too, Princess?" he asks as he continues to roll his hips while I resist the urge to wrap my legs around him. "You want to be the helpless victim. Overpowered. Dominated. Against your will. You like that non-con stuff."

I do. I'm not ashamed of it. Even men have non-con fantasies of being overpowered or emasculated. But I don't feel like admitting it right now.

"I'm the monster in your fantasies come to life," he continues. "I've got you captive in a remote cabin in the woods. There's no one here to rescue you, no one to stop me from doing whatever I want with you. You can be my little cum bucket for weeks on end. For me and all my friends."

In the little time I've been with Jack, my body seems to have developed a Pavlov's dog reaction to everything he says and does. The dirty talk is especially potent. My hips start to meet his rhythm.

"That's it," he says softly, "grind that slutty pussy against my cock. Because bad little girls like you enjoy being cum buckets. I can have cum pouring out of every hole of yours, even your nose and ears."

My ears burn, and my pussy throbs.

Grabbing my right buttock, he fits me tighter to him. "You can be a piss bucket, too, and start each morning off with a golden shower before you get fucked senseless."

I moan. Arousal presses against the boiling point. He was right to call bullshit on my refusal to come for him.

"Ever had two cocks in your pussy? How about two in your ass?"

Too distracted by the nearness of my orgasm, I don't answer till he slaps me. "No, sir."

"Then we'll be sure to try it. Maybe tonight. You don't need sleep, do you? Princess Slut would rather be fucked all night long."

I look into his eyes, helpless, and murmur, "I'm going to come..."

"Of course you are. I could make you hurt real bad, and you'd still come for me."

I come undone, spasming all over. Rapture washes over me, overwhelming the soreness of my nipples and the aching of my anus from Andrian's rough fucking.

Jack thrusts slowly, picking up speed when my climax ebbs. Grunting, he stabs into me to reach his own orgasm. We shiver in unison. I knew he'd succeed. He knew it too, and even though I lost, I'm happy.

Until he withdraws and says, "Now for your punishment, and this one is going to hurt bad."

I watch as he goes to a drawer and retrieves a set of leather cuffs. My heart stills when he opens a cabinet next. It's filled with electric play equipment: cables, an EMS box, zapper and Taser. I feel the blood drain from my face when he removes the cattle prod from its hook.

I'm not up for this. Especially without my safe word. Without thinking, I scramble off the bed and stand behind the headboard as if it can protect me.

He gives me an admonishing look. "Take your punishment like a good sub, Casey."

"I'll take my punishment, but can we do it later?" I ask.

"If you want it to be twice as long and twice as painful."

Normally I'm the rip-the-bandage-off-as-fast-as-possible kind of person, but that cattle prod intimidates me. I know I should want to get this punishment over sooner rather than later, but I need more prep.

He starts advancing toward me, so I quickly say, "I'll make it up to you. And your friend, too. I'll be a really good cum bucket."

"Of course you will. That's a given, with or without the punishment."

I don't like the sound of that. I assume he's saying that to play out this sexual fantasy we started, but it also sounds like he means it.

"I would be a very sorry Dom if I didn't follow through with your punishment," he tells me as he reaches the bed. Only its length separates us now.

I eye the cattle prod. "How badly does that thing hurt?"

He powers it up for a few seconds. It makes an ominous crackling sound. "It's worse than the zapper."

"You know from experience?"

He sets the cattle prod on the bed and walks toward me. "A responsible Dom always tests his equipment on himself."

"On a scale of one to ten, if the zapper is a five, what is the cattle prod?"

"For me it was an eight or nine."

Not the answer I wanted to hear. When he reaches for my wrists, I bolt. But for a man his size and strength, he's surprisingly fast and grabs me. I slip and fall to my knees. Grabbing my hair, he throws me against the headboard, harsh enough for the metal frame to bruise me. He cuffs my wrists to the bed. I have no choice but to submit. Getting the cattle prod, he powers it up. As it nears me, I whimper and attempt to crawl away from it. He touches it to my leg, and I shriek.

"That was a ten!" I cry.

"If you take your punishment like a good girl, maybe I'll let you come again."

Maybe?! I suppose it's better than sucking up the punishment without any possibility of a reward. And I have the feeling I'm getting punished no matter what. I do my best to stay still, but when the prod touches me again, my body wants to run as far away as possible.

"I'm sorry," I gasp between sobs of breath. "I can't do it. Not – not without help."

Squatting down, he grabs my ankle to hold my leg still while he runs the cattle prod along my thigh. I scream as the pain sears deep into my muscle. That was a fucking eleven or twelve! I want to cry.

Jack stands up and points the prod at my breast.

"Please, please, please," I babble as I strain away from the crackling ends.

The prod nears my nipple. Fear fills every inch of my body.

"I thought you wanted to be a good sub," he says. "You boasted you could be the best sub I've ever had."

It's hard for me to imagine anyone taking the cattle prod well, but thinking there might be a woman braver than me makes me jealous. I do want to be the best he's ever had.

Steeling my nerves and closing my eyes, I whisper, "Do it."

I wait for the electricity to stab me, but nothing happens. I open my eyes.

He withdraws the cattle prod. "We're going to try a different toy."

I've never felt so relieved in my life, though I don't know if this other toy is any better. But I am encouraged when he returns with a vibrator. He also has what looks like a large steel bullet plug with a circular base attached by a wire to an EMS device.

"Spread your legs," he directs.

I do as he commands. "I'm scared."

"We'll start off low."

Taking comfort in his gentler tone, I allow him to sink the metal dildo into me. True to his word, he starts off gradually. The currents in my pussy feel pleasurable. He turns it up to where the pleasure becomes discomfort. I squeal when the discomfort turns to pain, but it comes in waves, so I have a small window of reprieve before feeling like I'm getting caned inside my vagina.

He turns the setting higher. "Is this a ten out of ten?"

"Yes, yes, yes!" I cry as my body strains, feeling as if I could pull the bed apart. "Fuck!!"

"They can hear you all the way in Nevada."

"Sorry," I mumble.

"I've got something that can help with that." He returns with the dildo gag, explaining, "Since you won't be using your safe word."

Reluctantly, I open my mouth to receive the dildo. He buckles it around my head.

Setting down the control box, he tugs on the circular base of the shaft. Holy mother-fucker! Pain flares on the outside of my pussy. To my surprise, when he jams the dildo deeper, it feels better. I don't know how much more of this I can take, but then I hear the sweet, sweet sound of the vibrator. He nestles it at my clit, and it feels like the glorious gates of heaven have opened. The pain recedes as I revel in the delicious vibrations. I can actually come any second, but he starts pulling and pushing the base again. Pain and pleasure duel for dominance. My body doesn't know what to do with itself. Choosing pleasure, I put all my focus on the vibrator. My orgasm explodes through me, rattling me to my core. On that hard cement floor, I writhe and shake against the bed.

He removes the vibrator and turns the electricity down to a simmer. I shiver as he rubs my clit with his thumb. I don't think I've ever come this fast before. My head is still spinning when he puts the vibrator back on my clit. Does he want me to come again? If that's what he wants, my body will probably give it to him. He really does own it.

"We're going to go for a ten again," he informs.

Bile rises in my throat, but having a dildo in my mouth makes it hard to swallow. Adrenaline spikes through me when he cranks up the setting. I start panting like crazy till he lowers the setting back down, leaving nothing but pleasure. My orgasm comes on fast and strong again. If I were standing, it would have knocked me off my feet. How does he keep ripping these intense orgasms out of me?

After removing the electric plug, he caresses my pussy and clit, drawing out the last of my shivers. He kisses me on the top of the head. "You did good, princess."

It actually sounds like a term of endearment this time instead of one of derision. After putting everything away, he pulls on his sweatpants and heads upstairs. He isn't going to untie me first? But I'm too exhausted to make a fuss. My body has just been through hell and back, and I am grateful for the peace and quiet.

Chapter Twenty-Two

Kai

I left Casey cuffed to the bed because I wasn't feeling generous. And because I know she appreciates a Dom who is less forgiving. I don't like the conflicting emotions inside me right now. The only other times I've felt so conflicted was when I had to approve a brutal beating of one of my own men, a man whom I had liked, a man with family, but someone who had royally fucked up. The other time was after my adoptive parents had decided to adopt me. I didn't know whether or not to trust them. My adoptive father was going to have me beaten to a pulp for stealing from his wife, and I had no assurance that sentiment wouldn't return. Despite my fear, I had decided to place my trust in my new mother. I had been many years without a parent or guardian at that time, and her sweetness was something I didn't realize I was even starving for.

"What took you so long?" Andrian asks from where he sits on the living room sofa, shot glass in one hand and a cigar in the other. "Erectile problem?"

I join him on the sofa. "Teaching our princess a lesson."

"*Eto khorosho*. This slut, she is kinky, yes?"

I don't want to talk about it with Andrian. Looking at his cigar, I say, "Too much of that stuff will kill you."

"Everyone dies, eventually. You have been in America too long, my friend. You should consider going back and spending some time in Heihe or Blagoveshchensk."

"China's cracking down on smoking, too. And America's been my home for the majority of my life now."

"But we Russians and Chinese, we never forget our roots. We have centuries upon centuries of history and culture, not like Americans."

"My allegiance is to the *Jing San*."

Andrian nods in understanding. "You will be big man once we sell the HITDS."

Getting up, I call for Andy.

"I am ready to call Callaghan," Andrian says, "tell him he gives us laptop or we fuck his girl until she has no pussy left before we kill her."

The hair on my neck stands on end. "*Terpeniye*. We're going to go over the plans for the exchange first."

When Andy arrives, he outlines his two preferred locations he's evaluated for the exchange, a small remote beach on the far side of Angel Island and an abandoned warehouse outside East Palo Alto and near the Dumbarton Bridge.

"We can give Callaghan a choice between the two," Andy says. "Both have good sight lines."

"Fuck what Callaghan wants," Andrian spits as he gestures to Lev to pour him more vodka. "If he wants his little slut back, he will have to agree to our terms."

"We can monitor entry points better at the warehouse, but we can hide our secondary better on the island."

A broad grin spreads across Andrian's face. "Yes, I like the surprise. First, exchange. Then we kill fucking bastard."

"No one messes with us," Andy confirms.

Andy goes over the timing, who we will bring into the exchange and who will comprise the secondary, and contingencies if Callaghan tries to pull something. I've already heard and approved Andy's plans, but one thing I didn't consider earlier was the fact that Casey will likely be with her father when we riddle him with bullets.

"Is good," Andrian says of Andy's plan. He checks his Rolex. "Is not too late to call Callaghan."

"We call him tomorrow," I say, "when we're ready to move. Calling him tonight will just give him more time to plan."

Leaving Andy to wrap up the details involving Andrian's men, I head to the kitchen, where I get more water for Casey and head back downstairs.

Sitting on the floor, she leans with her eyes closed against the bedframe. I squat down before her to remove the dildo-gag.

"I thought you weren't going to come back till the morning," she says.

I uncuff her, then hand her the water.

"You want anything else to drink? Something to eat?" I ask.

She shakes her head.

"What did you think of the electroplay?"

"Intense."

"Did you want to use your safeword?"

"Hell, yes!"

"Would you want to do more electroplay?"

She thinks for a moment. "Yes. But maybe not the cattle prod. That thing is frightening."

Imagining what else I can do with Casey warms my body. I stand up and give her a hand to her feet.

She sits on the bed to finish her water, then looks at me carefully. "Was it your plan all along to invite your friend Andrian over?"

"No."

"So he was just in the neighborhood?"

"Something like that."

"I didn't know you were fluent in Russian."

"There's a lot you don't know about me, princess."

Her tone is serious. "Yeah, I'm getting that. Did your friend call you 'Kai?'"

"That's the name I grew up with."

"But you're called Jack now?"

Gazing at her, I wonder if I should just tell her the truth now. She's going to find out at some point soon. But I play with the idea of waiting till the very end. I don't think Andrian's done with her. Right now, however reluctant, she's consenting to Andrian. That will change once she realizes all of this isn't a fantasy.

"To you, it will always be 'Sir,'" I answer, sitting down next to her.

She studies me. "I can't decide if you're a good Dom or not. I mean, the orgasms are out of this world. To the point where I'm *exhausted*. That's never happened to me before. But...you're pushing it with Vladimir."

"Andrian," I correct.

"He staying the night?"

"Yes."

"Am I going to see more of him?"

"Yes."

She pouts. Part of me likes that she's not so keen on Andrian.

"You'd really let the fucker hit me?" she demands.

I feel the tug to reassure her, but that won't do her any good in the long run. "I'm not a knight in shining armor, remember? If you don't want to see his temper, stop antagonizing him."

"So he's the only one allowed to dish it?"

"You want to go at it with Andrian, be prepared for the consequences. Just don't expect a man to come to the rescue. Damsels in distress should learn to defend themselves."

"You'd let me defend myself? I wouldn't be considered a bad sub if I decided to punch your comrade?"

I think for a moment. We're not in a Total Power Exchange, but we didn't set the boundaries of our scenes and her fantasy. It hadn't mattered to me at the beginning to do so.

"If he tries to hurt you, do what you want," I allow, "but making him angrier is a risky move."

Andrian beat a prostitute once because she didn't speak any Russian and didn't understand what he wanted her to do. He was drunk at the time, but I don't think the absence of vodka would have made a huge difference.

I cup Casey's chin tenderly. "Don't you like being made a whore?"

"He rubs me the wrong way. It takes me out of the fantasy. Playing a slut in a scene is different than doing it in reality. I don't mind being *your* slut. I just don't want to be his."

I don't know why her words sound so good to me. Not needing to hear more, I claim her mouth, then ravage it. I like kissing her.

More than I should.

Chapter Twenty-Three

Casey

I wake spooned in Jack's arms, liking the warmth of his body more than I should, and it's not just because it's cool down here and I miss my down comforter. The basement's not as cold as it's been, though, so maybe the temperature got turned up at some point.

Hearing his steady breathing, I lay still so as not to wake him. Still tired, I consider going back to sleep. It might not even be morning for all I know. The basement is pitch dark. But I'm still unsettled by yesterday. I was glad to hear that he'd let me defend myself against Andrian. I don't want to be a damsel in distress relying on a man to save her. I'd love to kick Andrian in the nuts. But he's bigger and stronger. Would Jack—or Kai—really just stand by and do nothing?

Did I misjudge him completely? I think back to the moments when doubt crept into me, when I felt I might come to regret this kidnapping fantasy. There were times I felt as if Jack was warning me about that and even trying to prove his point. I thought I was being daring and adventurous. Maybe I was just being reckless. I put my trust in a man I barely knew. I let my attraction to him overpower anything else.

Maybe a more sensible woman would have stopped trusting Kai—that name suits him better than Jack—a long time ago. What if I had put my foot down about the electroplay? That shit had me freaked out. Would he have forced it on me? Somehow, I still had trust in him, even though a part of my brain was telling me I shouldn't. I trusted he would take me to the edge but not send me over the cliff to my death. And for that, I feel as if I've given him a piece of me that I can't take back. Maybe I don't want it back.

But there's something off with this Andrian guy. What exactly is the nature of the relationship between these guys? Why does Kai put up with this asshole? Are they lovers or something?

Jack shifts behind me. His morning wood brushes up against my ass. Desire perks within me. I nestle closer to him, an invitation. His hand caresses my thigh, then slips to my groin. He kisses me softly on the ear and then my neck. Remembering how his mouth had devoured mine last night, I arch my body into his. I want more of those kisses. I want for our lips to be joined, our bodies to lock together.

He rubs me between the legs, teasing me, making me yearn. New wetness flows over the stickiness there. I can't wait for him to be inside me. While pressing his hardness against my backside, he seals his mouth to my neck. My body is quick to burn, and I shove my ass to his pelvis. I don't care which hole he takes. I just want him to fuck me soon.

His hand taunts my clit, grazing it when he knows perfectly well how to clamp down. I open my mouth to tell him what I want, but I kind of like the silence. It's like we're trying to get away with something, like teenagers secretly making out in a movie theater. Staying quiet except for the occasional moan, I writhe against him and let his caresses drive me crazy. But I want to drive him just as crazy. I want to be the best fuck he's ever had.

Abruptly turning around, I kiss him quickly from his chest to his torso, licking his six-pack. He has the perfect body in my opinion. His tan is faded, but it's so much better than my winter paleness. Maybe I should have fit in a trip to Hawaii during the break.

Reaching for his hard-on, I go down on him. He groans and lets me blow him. I suck as long and hard as I can, relishing the way his cock flexes in my mouth. Moving up and down, I make sure as much of my tongue as possible drags along his shaft. I lick the underside of his crown until he fists a hand in my hair, then swallow him as deeply as I can while I squeeze his balls.

Given how much I crave him inside of me, I should probably stop, but I want to make him come. I want to feel some ownership over him, too. I want him to desire me at least half as much as I desire him. Pushing past my gag reflex, I take all of him. He lifts his hips, thrusting lightly. His hand tightens in my hair. With my free hand, I touch myself. I love going down on him and wonder what it would be like if we switched roles for a scene. Would he let me use the electroplay equipment on him? Maybe I'd pay him back a little for letting in Andrian.

Kai groans. *That's it. Come in me.*

I sink my fingers into my pussy, but it's nowhere near as good as having his cock.

"You're going to make me come, princess," he warns.

Briefly coming off him, I grin impishly. "A girl's got to start the day off with a good breakfast."

I gaze into his eyes, showing him how hungry I am before going back down on him. He presses his cock into my throat. I tug at his scrotum. My fingers find his perineum. My cheeks are sore from sucking, but I don't stop. I want my win/triumph.

A few minutes later, I reach my goal. His body tenses. Warm, tangy semen fills my mouth while he roars. I drink it down, milking every last drop from his flexing, pulsing cock. Having claimed my win, I climb up his body and ravage his mouth, making him taste himself on me while I hump his thigh. Grabbing me, he rolls me onto my back and sinks his fingers into me.

I gasp. He's touching the back of my clit, inside me. His thumb rubs my outer clit.

"Fuck, that feels good," I murmur.

He smiles as his gaze locks with mine. His fingers curl in and out. My jaw drops at how much pressure can build inside me. It's like my desire is a ten-ton weight, waiting to be released.

"Can I come?" I remember to ask.

When he doesn't respond right away, I worry. I can't not come. Not when it feels this incredible. My orgasm is coming at me like a runaway freight train, and there's no stopping it.

He intensifies his motions, his fingers making sloshing, squishing sounds as he pounds into my pussy. Tension grips my lower body. I probably should have asked to go to the bathroom because I have that sensation.

Please let me come.

"I'm going to count down from ten," he says, "then you can come."

"I don't know if—"

"Ten...nine..."

Okay, okay. I'll hold it. Right now I can't tell if I'm going to come or piss. Or both.

"...eight...seven."

I whimper.

"Six."

Hurry!

"Five...four..."

Fuck, fuck, fuck.

"Three."

Oh no.

"Two..."

One!!!

"One."

My body bursts into spasms, euphoria racking me from head to toe. I can't tell if I clenched hard enough not to accidentally pee. I pulse everywhere. With rapture. With relief.

When I finally find my breath, which still shakes, I say, "Thank you, Sir. I thought I was going to pee on the bed. I didn't, did I?"

"Next time, don't fight your body," he replies.

"You *want* me to piss the bed?"

"Sometimes that sensation is the precursor to squirting. You wanted to squirt, didn't you?"

I had said that. He remembered. I love that he listens to me, how he doesn't seem to miss anything, how he takes in what I want and gives it to me. Even though he doesn't seem to regard 'princesses,' he's doing his fair share of spoiling me. For several seconds, we're both silent. We just stare. He probably sees the gratitude—maybe something more. A muscle along his jaw ripples. He seems vaguely uncomfortable for a moment.

"I'd love for you to make me squirt," I say in a seductive voice, lightening the moment.

But before he can respond, another voice cuts in.

"Starting without me?"

Chapter Twenty-Four

Kai

Fuck. I was so into what I was doing with Casey, I had forgotten about Andrian for the moment.

He continues down the stairs. When he approaches, I can smell the cigarette he's already smoked. He has on a tank and track pants. Looking Casey over, he starts rubbing his crotch. Instinctively, I want to put myself between them.

"I have breakfast for *shlyukha*," Andrian says.

"I ate already," Casey replies.

Andrian smirks. "Do I care?"

He pulls out his cock. Casey looks to me. I gaze back at her. *What are you expecting? You know what a good sub should do.*

Disgruntled by her lack of movement, Andrian turns to me. I grab her hair and guide her toward Andrian, telling her, "Make Daddy proud."

Her reluctance thaws and she reaches for Andrian's cock. She pumps it several times before enveloping it with her mouth.

He pushes her head down, forcing her to take more of him. "So, you are daddy-girl, yes?"

Casey makes no reply and only continues to blow him.

Pressing her head to his crotch, Andrian whips out his cell. "How about we take photo to send to daddy so he can see his girl is slut."

At the sound of a click, Casey pushes herself off Andrian. "Did you just take a photo of me?"

He takes another shot. "Next, I take photo of cum all over your face."

"What the hell? I didn't say you could take photos."

Intervening, I say to Andrian, "Delete the photos."

Andrian only stares at me. "Why?"

"I didn't say photos are allowed."

"Why no?"

"Photos aren't needed. Besides, what if Elena sees them on your phone?"

"Elena is never allowed to touch my phone."

"Just delete the fucking photos."

"And will be fun to watch Callaghan's face when he sees—"

Casey pipes up, "What?"

I grab the phone from Andrian. He tries to grab it back, but I deflect his arm.

"You going to delete the photos?" I ask.

"Fuck you," Andrian replies.

I throw the phone across the room, smashing it against the wall. I know the photos still exist in the cloud, but the phone was an MX-900. I know the software and have contacts with hackers who can access all of Andrian's saved data.

"*Chert poberi,*" Andrian curses.

I dodge the right hook he throws at me, grab his arm, pin it behind his back and shove him into the wall.

"I said no pictures," I growl.

Feeling him relent, I back off him. He turns to stare at me, confused and angry.

"What the hell?" he asks in Russian.

"Put your dick away," I tell him.

His jaw clenched, he stares at me, probably contemplating whether or not to take me on. In all our years, we've never fought. We've argued. Andrian once struck me when I tried to pull him off an asshole before Andrian beat him to death for double-crossing us, but other than that, we got along better than most married couples.

In Russian, I say, "We should focus on the exchange, make the call now and get this shit done with."

Andrian looks to Casey and replies in Russian, "And if Callaghan doesn't cooperate, then we fuck her up good."

"Go. I'll be up in a minute."

Pulling up his pants, Andrian grabs his busted phone from the floor and heads upstairs.

Once he's gone, Casey asks, "How does he know my name?"

I put on my own pants. "What are you talking about?"

"He just said 'Callaghan.'"

"So?"

"What did he say?"

"That he wanted to fuck you later," I answer non-chalantly. "You want a shower?"

"Yes! I've had cum oozing out of me for hours. But what was all that shit with the photos? He said he was going to send them to my dad."

"That turn you on?"

"No! Gross! But he said—"

"You want this shower or not?"

"I do, but—"

"Then enough with the talking."

I throw her over my shoulder and start heading up the stairs. I take her all the way to my bedroom, which has a ten-foot wide fireplace and expansive windows looking out onto the Sierra Nevada.

"You had me sleeping in the basement while this was your room?" Casey exclaims.

I set her down in the bathroom. "You can take a bath or shower. Your choice."

She practically drools as she looks at the giant bath-tub set in an alcove with floor-to-ceiling windows. I throw her a towel, then step out, closing the door behind me. I could use a shower, too, and a shave.

But if I stick around, she's going to throw a bunch of questions at me. I can see the wheels in her mind turning. I head to my closet.

"It's me," Andy says through the door after knocking.

"Come in," I respond as I pick out a button-up shirt, black pants and matching jacket.

Entering, Andy closes the door behind him. He sets down a tray with tea on the dresser. "Andrian's pissed as hell you broke his phone. Kept asking me what was wrong with you, if maybe you were on drugs or something."

The *Jing San* deals plenty in drugs, but I've never touched the stuff.

"What'd you tell him?"

"'Or something.'"

Andy eyes me carefully as I dress. I know what he's assessing me for.

He glances toward the bathroom. "She in there?"

"Taking a bath. She's going to need some clothes."

"For what?"

She would look more pathetic in her torn school-girl-slut outfit, and I do want to inflict pain on

Callaghan. But Casey's been through enough. I say to Andy, "We're not handing her back to her father butt naked. You're the smallest among us. You have anything she can wear?"

"I'll check."

"Then get ready for the call with Callaghan."

"What about her?"

"Bring up some breakfast. She can stay in my room. Put Tao or someone at the door so she doesn't go wandering."

Andy nods and heads out. I stand there listening to the water running into the bathtub. It would have been nice to join her in the bath, but I've got to stop thinking like that. She can tell something is off, and it's time her fantasy bubble got popped. If all goes according to plan, she'll be back with her father in less than twelve hours.

Only she won't have a father for long. And she might end up collateral damage herself.

Chapter Twenty-Five

Casey

As I sit in the tub and stare out the window at clear blue skies—a gorgeous day to hit the mountains—I think back to when I first saw Jack. He felt mysterious and a touch dangerous. Most women can only fantasize about being with a man like that. I made it happen.

But now that he feels a tad less mysterious and more dangerous, I wonder if maybe I made a mistake. I'm grateful he stopped his friend from taking pics of me. I was surprised he broke Andrian's cellphone and didn't seem the least bit remorseful. It's not that I mind having pictures taken of me naked. I've sent several to past boyfriends. But I don't like having them taken without my consent.

And what had Andrian said he was going to do with the pics? Send them to my dad? Why? He spoke with too much earnestness for me to think he was just goofing around. And it didn't sound like some weird kink he had. It was like he wanted to make my dad miserable, like he knew my dad. But that would be a crazy coincidence, right?

After getting out of the tub, I wrap myself in a plush towel. I don't feel like blow-drying my hair at the moment, so I step into the bedroom to see if Kai is there. He isn't. Instead, I find a serving cart with what turns out to be breakfast accompanied by a note.

Help yourself to food and clothes on bed.

I pick up a slice of bacon and gnaw on it. It's good bacon. The clothes on the bed appear to be a man's shirt and sweats. They don't seem like Jack's size.

I really want to talk to him and make it plain to him in private that Andrian is a hard limit. I was okay blowing him this morning as part of my slut fantasy, but I didn't like the look in his eyes when he was taking pics of me. I didn't need Jack to tell me that Andrian has a temper, and I fully believe that Andrian is capable of hurting me. While some women find that kind of raw, untamed, beastly quality sexy, it doesn't make me feel safe. Jack, on the other hand, has control, which allows me to be more adventurous.

I would rather he choose to defend me if Andrian tried anything, but Jack's right that women shouldn't expect men to come to the rescue. Hannah would swoon whenever a guy in a movie or story would step in to prevent the heroine from being raped by some jerk, but I like heroines who can kick ass themselves.

And Jack did stop Andrian from taking photos of me. He didn't have to do that. I forgot to thank him, too.

I down some coffee and decide to see if Jack is nearby. But when I open the door, a man not Jack stands there.

"Um, hi," I greet.

The man doesn't speak or move.

"Jack around?" I ask.

"Boss is busy," he answers.

I make an attempt to look around him, but he blocks my path. Who is this guy, and what is he trying to do?

"Will he be back?" I try.

The guy shrugs and continues to stand there as if he's glued to the floor. I wait to see if he goes anywhere. He doesn't.

"Are you camping out here?" I inquire.

He says nothing. He referred to Jack as 'Boss.' What does this guy do for Jack?

"Would you mind finding Jack and letting him know I want to talk to him?" I ask.

"Not my job."

"Okay. Remind me to file a customer service complaint."

Part of me wants to test him and see if he moves when I try to walk past him, but I've only got a towel on. I decide to close the door and wait to hear if the man will leave. He doesn't.

What the hell?

I open the door and say to the guy, "Look, I'd really like to talk to Jack right now."

"He's busy."

"What if I want to see for myself?"

His gaze sweeps over me as if to ask, "Wearing that?"

I flush. Screw it. I've had half a dozen guys not just see me naked but fuck me. I don't care that I only have a towel on.

But when I try to walk past the guy, he blocks me and reiterates, "He's busy."

"Busy with what? His girlfriend show up or something?"

"Why don't you go back in the room and wait?"

It's a rhetorical question. He's telling me what I should do. I get the feeling this guy would wrestle me if he had to. Relenting, I go back inside. He closes the door for me.

I start pacing. I don't like this. Where did Jack go, and why is there a guard preventing me from seeing him?

Deciding I want to test the guard again, I go over to the change of clothes but turn around when I hear the bedroom door open. Jack walks in. Damn, he looks hot in that dark suit. Something's different in the way that he looks at me. He feels distant.

I go up to him. "Who's that man standing outside the door?"

"No one you need to worry about," Jack replies.

"He's like a jail-keeper or something. He wouldn't let me go looking for you. Why?"

"I was busy."

There's an edge to all his responses. Does he think I'm being too nosy?

"Jack, what's going on?" I ask.

"We're taking you back home—*I'm* taking you back. Today."

Okay. I'm disappointed at the abrupt end to my time here, but it's probably for the best.

"So eat your breakfast and get dressed," he finishes tersely.

"What's your problem?" I demand, not liking the way this is ending. After putting up with his comrade, I deserve a nicer farewell.

He narrows his eyes. "What do you mean?"

"We're done. I get it. You don't have to be a jerk about it."

He shakes his head to himself. "I've been called worse."

"I haven't."

"Of course you haven't. *Princess.*"

It's like he wants to pick a fight. And if that's where he wants to go, I'm not afraid. I step into him. "You know, it was kind of fun being called a slut or a whore, but 'princess' not so much. What do you have against me anyway? Or do you just have a chip on your shoulder when it comes to anyone who doesn't have the same rags to riches story you do?"

A muscle along his jaw tenses, and I second-guess my decision to challenge him.

But all he says is, "Get dressed."

It's the sensible thing to do, but I'm done submitting to him. "If we're finished, you're not my Dom anymore. You don't get to tell me what to do."

He closes what remains of the gap between us, and I immediately feel a current go through me. Damn my body. It can't help but react to him.

He lowers his head. "You need someone to do it for you, princess?"

Pursing my lips, I refuse to be intimidated, though I wouldn't put it past him to take me home wearing nothing but a towel if I pass up the chance to dress.

I tilt my head. "You plan on getting your buddy Andrian to do it?"

His eyes constrict.

I press on. "'Course, Andrian would probably want to do something else first. Would that turn you on? Maybe I should go get him. We could have one last encore..."

I turn to walk past him. He could easily call my bluff. I thought I made it obvious that I don't like Andrian, but I wanted to see if there was the least bit of jealousy in Jack.

He grabs me by my arm and throws me onto the bed before pinning his body over mine.

Gripping my jaw in one hand, he demands. "Is that what you want, princess? Andrian won't refuse. Maybe this time I'll let him take his pics."

Although I'm glad Jack stopped me, his words aren't the ones I wanted to hear. He does sound a little angry at my suggestion to get Andrian, which is a good sign, I think, but Jack might make me see my bluff through. Would he really let his dick of a friend take pictures of me?

"Asshole," I spit as I try to push Jack off me.

"What's the matter? You didn't have any problems getting off on any of my men. How is Andrian any different?"

I try wriggling from under Jack, but that only causes the towel to come undone. I pause, conscious of my naked body squirming against him. Our gazes lock as heat flares within me. I see desire swimming in his eyes, too. I shouldn't want this. But I do. So very bad.

Chapter Twenty-Six

Kai

Feeling her writhing beneath me, pressing against me in her fruitless, half-hearted attempt to escape me, I grow hot with desire. Fast. When I first saw Casey, I found her attractive, but there wasn't this burning need to claim her, to possess her. Somehow she got under my skin, and now I want nothing more than to smother her lips with mine, to sink into her depths with my cock. Even though she's pissed at me, I know I can get her to spread her legs willingly for me. My hand reaches to grope her breast to show her that.

"So we're not done?" she asks with an arched brow. She bucks her hips at me. "You want more of this?"

"I'm taking more, yes," I reply.

"What if I don't want to give you more?"

I smile. "This part of your non-con fantasy? You want me to take you by force?"

Her breath becomes uneven as she stares into my gaze. I see some hesitation and a lot of arousal. I know she likes to play with reluctance.

"You want me to be the big, bad, evil dragon," I continue, grabbing her buttock and grinding her to my hardening cock, "ravishing the helpless princess."

"What happens after the dragon takes his fill?"

"He sends her back to her castle, back to the king and queen."

"Is that the happily ever after?"

I feel a spot of wetness seep through my pants where her pussy rubs against me. "Yes. The princess never encounters the dragon again and marries a nice Irish prince."

"What if she decides she likes the dragon better?"

A vein in my neck throbs. I warn her, "She wouldn't be that stupid. The king would never approve."

"Yeah, he'd probably send his army after the dragon."

"She should stick with the prince."

"She doesn't want the shitty prince. She wants the *dragon*."

Her response heats my blood and exasperates me at the same time. She's relentless because she doesn't have a clue. Maybe I should give her one. An act of tough love.

I flip her onto her stomach, pull her till her ass rounds the edge of the bed, and yank her arms behind her back. Bending them, I pin them down with my left hand while I undo my belt and pants with my right. Her pussy has got to be sore from all the sex she's had, but she's wet. I plunge in, swift and deep, making her cry out. I thrust hard and rough. She starts dropping F-bombs.

"You know that the dragon's just using the princess for sex," I growl. "And when he's done with her, she's going to be a broken, cum-soaked mess."

Casey grunts out, "Maybe she's okay with that."

I stop. There are few people whom I don't believe I can prevail against. Maybe Raphael Lee, whom I regard as my older brother, because he's cooler than ice. Shen Lee might be another, because the son of the triad head could sneak up on a puma and kill faster than a Komodo dragon. But that's it.

So why do I feel like I'm getting nowhere with Casey Callaghan? Is she that thick-headed? That masochistic?

I resume pounding into her, my body slamming into her so fast and strong she can't utter a decent scream. This might be more painful than pleasurable for her, but it's what she wants. Her knuckles turn white as she digs her fingers into her palms. I've never anger fucked before. I don't know if I'm angry at her or myself.

My orgasm explodes, shaking my whole body. Slowing down, I opt for a deeper penetration as my cum empties into her. After a final violent shudder, I withdraw. I release her. She trembles and grasps the bed linen.

Shit. I was too rough with her. Hearing her sniffle, I turn her over to see if she's crying. Her eyes are wet, but she looks...triumphant.

Staring at her in surprise and awe, I want to apologize. I haven't felt this repentant since my early days with my adoptive parents. Unsure exactly what they had planned for me, I had once attempted to steal a few household items that had looked expensive to me. My father discovered it and had me whipped with a belt.

I have something Casey will like better than an apology. Spreading her legs, I settle between her thighs and part her labia with my fingers to access her clit with my tongue. She moans receptively. Gently, I lick her. The scent of her, the taste of her intrudes my senses. I wish I had withheld my ejaculation. I flick my tongue over her swollen nub, making her writhe and whimper. It doesn't take her long to come. I suck her pulsing clit till she squeals.

"Okay, okay!" she pants.

Straightening, I position myself on the bed next to her and caress her mound and abdomen, occasionally dipping my hand between her legs. She shivers and looks at me with bright, glossy eyes. My chest tightens. Lowering herself, I smother her mouth with mine. She threads her fingers through my hair and pulls. Hard. If this kiss were a duel between the dragon and the princess, I wouldn't necessarily bet on the dragon.

I slide a finger into her battered but extremely slick pussy. She grunts but doesn't push me away.

"Does it hurt?" I check. "Your pussy bruised?"

"Yeah," she acknowledges. "Bet a real princess wouldn't be able to take it."

Is she trying to prove to me how tough she is? She doesn't have to.

I add a second finger, feeling for her most sensitive spot. Her body rises when I find it. She gasps softly as I gently stroke her there. We stop kissing so that she can focus on my fondling. Her breath quivers. She releases a shaky laugh, then a whimpering moan. Her fingers tighten in my hair. Our brows touch. I drink it all in, not wanting it to stop. Like a bottle of Stoli Elit or a run down Sea Bowl at Palisades Tahoe, this feels heady and intoxicating.

"Oh, fuck," she softly whines. "I'm going to..."

"To what?" I ask. "Come?"

She furrows her brow and looks worried. "Maybe..."

"You're going to come good for me, princess. I want you to squirt all over me."

"How?"

"By releasing. Let it go."

"What if I piss?"

"If you piss, you piss."

I quicken my motions, making sure I hit her clit while I stroke her G-spot.

"Fuck!" she cries.

A moment later, I withdraw my fingers and a small stream of liquid follows. I jam my fingers back into her and pull out a few more sprays.

"Oh, fuck, oh, fuck," she says, her body trembling. "Did I just pee on your bed?"

"You squirted on my bed."

Sighing with relief, she runs a hand through her hair, then smiles broadly at me.

"That was fucking awesome," she tells me, with a starry-eyed look as if I just gave her her first orgasm. "Thank you."

My cock has started to harden again, but I stand up and redo my pants. "I'm sorry I went so hard."

"You made up for it."

And maybe I shouldn't have. I just undid the intention behind the rough fucking. It's not characteristic of me to do an about-face like that.

I give her a hand up. "Get dressed. It's time to return the princess to her castle."

She sits up but doesn't reach for the clothes. "Does the dragon ever come back?"

"Not after tonight."

"Why not?"

"It's for the best."

"How about an encore? Just once? I've got to go back to Notre Dame soon, so you don't have to worry that I'll be around stalking you or anything."

You're not going to want an encore after what goes down tonight, is what I want to say.

"No. We're done."

Standing up, she grabs the lapels of my sports jacket and presses her body into mine. "But why should the fun stop? You're a good Dom, I'm a good sub. And you like me. You know how I can tell?"

She grabs my crotch. My cock stirs closer to her grasp.

"I think you should let the dragon play again," she says.

Firmly, I push her away. "That's enough."

"If you want, I'm open to other stuff. If you like your comrade so much, I'll even—"

"No!" I growl. "You got your fantasy. The end."

She narrows her eyes at me. "What are you afraid of?"

I don't answer her. The truth is, I'm afraid she might not live to see tomorrow.

Chapter Twenty-Seven

Casey

When he doesn't answer my question, I try to prompt him. "You're not afraid of having too much fun, are you?"

He scowls. "Grow up. There's more to life than fun."

"Like what? Making more money? Because it's not enough that you have a big ass house, own a gorgeous cabin in Tahoe, and drive a Bugatti? Oh wait, it's about honor. But is it? Or is it more about flexing?"

His features darken. "A hedonistic princess who hasn't worked a day in her life wouldn't understand. You don't know anything."

I bridge the distance between us again. "I know we're good together. I know we have chemistry. I

don't see why we can't have a little more fun together."

I reach for his crotch, but he stops my hand.

"What are you so afraid of?" I ask. "That I'm gonna
develop feelings for you? Trust me, I'm not looking
for a relationship."

He looks unhappy, tense.

"Or are you worried about your own feelings?" I
tease.

"You have no clue what you're talking about. Now
get the fuck dressed."

Everything about his tone suggests that I should
just shut up and do as he says, but I feel like I'm on
to something. There's something between us, something beyond physical attraction even. I'm not willing
to give up on that.

"Not until you tell me what your problem is," I
declare.

"You're the one with the problem."

"Because I wasn't born into poverty like you? I get
that already. But you already knew that, so why did
you decide to hook up with me anyway?"

He frowns. He doesn't like my question. I use my free hand to play with a button on his shirt.

"You can admit that you like me," I tell him. "What's the big deal? I like you."

Gazing into his eyes, I glimpse something like torment in their depths.

He grabs my other hand. "Being a spoiled brat isn't your only problem."

"You can punish me for being a brat."

"If I had more time, trust me, I would."

"So why don't you? What's the rush? Can't a big guy like you make your own time?"

"That's your other problem, princess. You live in a fairy tale. You need to wake up to reality."

"What reality?"

I press my hips to him, prompting him to throw me off. I land sitting on the bed.

His frown becomes more grim. "You know what your father does for a living, princess?"

"Sort of," I reply as I wonder why we're talking about my father.

"Your father, Liam Callaghan, is a Mob Boss."

For several seconds, I only blink, trying to process how Jack knows this. Should I deny his accusation or will he see through me? Of course a guy like Jack would have the means to dig into my family background. Is that why he doesn't want to have anything to do with me now?

Undecided if I should try and dissuade him from the truth, I ask, "Why do you say that?"

"Because, baby, I'm triad."

He lets that sink in for me. I heard my father mention triad a few times after we moved to California. But what has that to do with me and Jack? Is he suggesting it wasn't a coincidence or a nice gesture of fate that we met at Club Voyeur?

"And Andrian, he's Bratva," Jack adds.

I stare at the floor as I process what this means. Glancing back up at Jack, I say, "Andrian knew about my father. *You* knew. From the beginning?"

"From the beginning."

"Then why...?"

"Your father stole something of mine, so I stole something of his."

My gaze digs into his. He means...me. So this was never about fulfilling a fantasy or spending time with me because he liked me. It was about a vendetta?

As if reading my mind, he confirms, "Is Princess finally catching on?"

Without thinking, I jump to my feet and slap him across the mouth. I'm tired of the condescending pet name.

"The name's not 'Princess,'" I seethe.

Unfazed by the slap, he replies, "Okay, Casey. Is that all you got?"

All this time, the connection I felt we had was just him leading me on. It wasn't about me. It was about my dad. I was something he 'stole,' fucked, and was about to throw away now that he's done using me.

Angry and scared, I grab the porcelain lamp off the bedside table to hurl at him. He blocks it, shattering the lamp.

I continue hitting him with what remains. "You fucking asshole!"

The door opens and the guard rushes in. "Boss?"

Jack grabs the lamp and wrests it from me. I try to resist but end up stumbling into the guard. I spot a gun beneath his blazer. Holy shit. He has a gun. Without thinking, I grab it from its holster and cock it. They freeze. I'm guessing the gun is loaded.

Hands shaking, I say, "I want to make a call."

"To whom?" Jack asks calmly.

"None of your fucking business. Just give me a damn phone."

"He's not there."

I pale. "Who?"

"Chase."

"Wh-What do you mean?"

"There's me, four of my men, Andrian, and two of his men. You're outnumbered, so the best thing for you—"

"Where's my bodyguard? Where's Chase?"

I guess the answer from his silence. Shit. Shit. Shit. Maybe Jack's lying. Maybe Chase is just incapacitated. Or still in San Francisco.

"You had this all planned out?" I nearly scream.

"You walked right into it. In fact, you set it up yourself."

I did?

I did. Fuck me. What I thought was the universe doing something nice for me turned out to be a cruel joke. And now I'm all alone—and fucking naked—in a cabin full of men who have done god knows what!

"You're going to get me a phone," I say with more calm than I feel, "and the keys to your car."

Jack looks me over and smirks. "You're leaving in your birthday suit? You should have dressed when you had the chance, princess."

"Shut up!"

"You're not going anywhere."

The shaking inside my body intensifies. "I thought we were done. End of story."

"It's the end of your fairy tale. Your dad gets to have you back when he returns what's rightfully mine."

This just gets worse.

"Too bad," I say. "I'm leaving, by myself if you don't want anyone to get shot."

"You're not shooting anyone."

"Try me. I happen to have really good aim."

He starts walking toward me, causing my nerves to explode with alarm.

"Stop!" I cry. "Stay the fuck where you are!"

"I'm giving you a better target."

"I *will* shoot you, asshole."

I can't believe I thought he was the Dom of my dreams. I can't believe I was falling for him.

"You're a spoiled princess who's lived all her life in an ivory tower," he says. "You don't have what it takes to pull the trigger."

"Fuck you."

Pull the trigger. Show the asshole. But do I really want to kill him? Maybe I'll just injure him?

I start to squeeze, but the gun flies out of my hand. Someone came in and kicked it from my grasp. Before I can evaluate if any of my fingers got broken, a pair of arms bear-hugs me from behind. I feel the pinch of a needle at my neck. Shit. What did they stick me with? I try to break free of the arms around me, but I know it's fruitless. Am I going to die?

The last thing I see before my vision blurs into darkness is Jack. When you play with dragons, chances are you'll get burned.

Chapter Twenty-Eight

Casey

When I drift awake, I can't see anything through the hood covering my head. My hands and feet are tied. I feel the rumble of a vehicle beneath my prone body. I might be in the van that I was 'kidnapped' in earlier. What I thought was a fake kidnapping turned out to be real. I don't feel naked, so I'm probably wearing the shirt and sweats that had been on the bed. But I've got bigger things to worry about than nudity...

The next time I wake up, the hood is pulled from my head. My mouth feels dry, and I think I've been drooling. I'm still lying on my side on some hard, metallic bed. The back of a cargo van. My vision comes into focus. Jack and a guy I don't recognize, though I think he might have been the one who kicked the gun out of my hands, kneel before me.

Triad. They're fucking triad. How am I going to get myself out of this?

Jack reaches for me to help me up, but I shirk from his grasp and flop back down on the floor.

"I'm going to untie your hands," he says, "so that you can have something to drink. If you try anything, you'll regret it. Simple as that."

I glare at him. There was a time when I liked being tied up by him, but that was a world away. A fairy tale, like he said. As much as I feel like my father failed me, he had done a fairly good job keeping his family life separate from the Mob. Till now.

I let Jack untie my wrists and hoist me into a sitting position. The other guy hands me a bottle of water. Jack watches me drink the water. I want to tear those eyes of his out. I feel so played, so used, so deceived. I can't believe I let him come inside me. Over and over again. I probably still have his junk inside me.

If only I hadn't been so blinded by lust. If only I hadn't been so damn attracted to him. How could I have known he was part of a criminal organization?

But I should have gotten to know more about him before I went off on this fantasy with him. I was too trusting, too naive, too careless. Everything Jack suggested I was. A princess who didn't know better.

"You don't have anything stronger?" I ask now that my mouth doesn't feel like dry cotton.

"We can get you a soda, but it's best to stay away from alcohol," Jack says.

I scoff. "Why? You don't think I can hold my liquor?"

"It's for your safety. The exchange we're going to do with your father is dangerous, especially if there are surprises. You don't want to be doing anything stupid."

"My safety matters to you?" I ask cynically.

"My father taught me to be tidy and avoid unnecessary damage and death."

A cold shiver goes through me at his last word. "Is there a chance I'll die?"

"Not if all goes according to plan. How trustworthy is your dad?"

"I don't know how my dad conducts business."

"You don't have any clue?"

At twelve, I found out that our family was Mob when I overheard my mother and father arguing one night. I didn't fully comprehend the extent of my father's dealings then and I didn't want to know more. For years after, I simply ignored the realities around my father's line of "work." I pretended we were a normal family. As Jack said, I lived in a fairy tale.

"No," I answer. "I figured the less I know the better."

"But your brother is involved. Isn't this a family business?"

"I don't know the ins and outs of what my father does. All I'm good for is marrying Kenton so we can grow the family business with a bunch of in-laws."

Kai appraises me as if trying to decide whether or not to believe me. "So you don't know if your father ever pulled a fast one or backstabbed on a deal?"

"If I did, why would I tell you?" I return. I have no loyalty toward the Mob, but as angry as I feel toward my dad, I can't betray him. I decide to turn Kai's question back on him. "How trustworthy are *you*?"

"I'm straight with those who are straight with me."

"So all my dad has to do is give you back some computer or something?"

"That's correct."

I stare at him closely. "And that's it?"

"Like I said, the princess gets to return home and never has to see the dragon again."

"And no one has to get hurt?"

"As long as there are no surprises. Otherwise, I can't guarantee anything."

Jack's jacket is unbuttoned, and I see a holster with a gun tucked beneath his left arm. "Do I get one of those?"

He lifts a brow. "You're asking me to arm the enemy?"

From lover to enemy in less than twenty-four hours. Fuck me.

"You...you use that often?" I ask of the gun.

"No," he says gently, as if to reassure me.

I'm not reassured and follow up with, "When was the last time you used it—or any gun?"

"Not including practice, I assume."

"Not including practice," I confirm.

"It's been a while. Two years or so."

"Is that because you have men to do the...the killing for you?"

Without flinching, he replies, "Yes."

"Have you ever—?"

"I don't think you want to be asking these kinds of questions. You might not be happy with the answer."

Needing something to relax the spike in agitation within me, I ask, "Can I get a cigarette?"

Jack nods to the other guy, who opens the door and hops out. I see that it's pitch black outside before the door closes. How long was I out?

"Where are we?" I ask.

"Back in San Francisco."

I take a small amount of solace in the fact that we're back in the Bay Area. I wonder if my father might be near and if there's a way I can escape. There's no way I can get past Jack—if that's his real name—and his men, who I'm guessing are not too far. I need more time to think.

"So you're not really some import-export business-man," I say. "I'm guessing Jack isn't your real name."

"It's Kai. Kai Lee."

He'd tell me his real name? Maybe it's just another fake.

"I'm not worried you'll go to the cops," he explains. "You can't implicate me without implicating your father."

I lift my chin. "Maybe I don't care if I do. My father isn't going to win any parent-of-the-year awards."

"You won't have any evidence to back up your claims."

I don't dispute him. Besides, I don't want him to worry that I'll make trouble for him and give him any reason to want to dispose of me.

"So Kai's your real name? You're actually being honest with me?"

He hasn't been forthcoming with me since the day we met. Why should I believe anything he says? Every moment we had together turned out to be a charade. I was nothing but bait to him, something he could take and use as leverage against my father. A part of me feels like crying. Because I'm scared. Because my dream turned into a nightmare.

Jack—Kai must see my distress, because he says, "I'm sorry."

His words actually make me want to cry more, but there's no way I'm going to let this asshole see my tears.

That a cool and hardened criminal even knows the word 'sorry' surprises me, but I snap back bitterly, "That supposed to make it all better?"

"No," he acknowledges.

His man returns with a pack of Treasurers. Where did he get cigarettes like this so quickly?

My hand shakes as I hold one to my mouth. The guy lights it for me. I draw in the nicotine and wait for a calm that doesn't come. I inhale again, but I feel sick to my stomach. I'm too agitated for the cigarette to work well. I probably have to smoke the whole pack to calm myself.

"When is the exchange happening?" I ask. "When do I get to see my father?"

"In about an hour."

That sounds like forever.

"I need to pee," I lie.

Kai and his man exchange glances. Kai says to me, "You can piss behind the van."

Both men get up.

"Aren't you going to untie my ankles first?" I ask.

Kai sweeps me into his arms and carries me out the van. I could try to gouge his eyes out right now, but I wouldn't get very far. And this guy knows how to make one pay.

Outside the van, I see we're near a dock on the Marin County side of the Bay. I can see the twinkle of the city and the lights on the Golden Gate Bridge. I welcome the familiar sight, glad that we're not somewhere remote where Kai can dump our bodies.

After he sets me down, I drop the cigarette and grind it out. I need to gather my thoughts. Should I just let this exchange happen and hope for the best? Should I plead for mercy? Or should I look for opportunities to escape?

"I thought you needed to pee," Kai says.

Realizing I was busy assessing my surroundings, I check to see who's around. There's just us. Even though it's dark, I ask, "Some privacy?"

Kai turns around.

I exhale, pull down the sweatpants and hope I can produce a tinkle. I honestly might be too scared to pee.

While I do my best to relax enough to go, I hear a voice that makes me tense all over.

It's Andrian.

Chapter Twenty-Nine

Kai

What's taking her so long to piss?

Hearing Andrian, I turn to Andy. "Keep an eye on her."

Walking around to the other side of the van, I greet Andrian.

"Nikita, Dmitri, Lev and Peter are in position," Andrian tells me. "As soon as exchange is done, no more Callaghan, no more Mob."

Recalling the fear in Casey's eyes, I rub the back of my neck. "About that. Let's just do the exchange."

Andrian looks as if he doesn't believe what he's hearing. "Just exchange? What about Callaghan?"

"We can take care of him later."

"Why not tonight? We have perfect opportunity."

"Collateral damage."

"What collateral damage? You mean the girl?"

"Yes."

"Callaghan must pay. Is message to anyone thinking to steal from us."

"That can be addressed later," I reiterate.

Andrian frowns, then rubs his jaw. "*Deystvitel'no?* You worried about little *pizda*? You are not done fucking her? You want pussy, I get you best pussy—Russian pussy."

Andrian knows damn well I can get my own Russian pussy.

"I'll plan and execute the hit if you don't want to be bothered," I offer.

"Watching that son of a bitch bleed to death is best part! There will not be better chance than tonight."

I can't argue that we're not well set up tonight to take out Callaghan, and we probably aren't going to get a better shot at the guy. But I stay firm. "Later. If we can't get it done, you can have a larger share of the proceeds when we sell HITDS."

That doesn't seem to make Andrian happier, but he asks, "How much?"

"An extra ten percent."

He weighs the offer. "Fuck. But only for you, Kai."

Shaking his head, he walks away to the boats that will take him and his men to Angel Island.

I return to the other side of the van where Andy and Casey are standing. I assume she's had her chance to pee.

"Need another cigarette?" I ask her.

She shakes her head.

I say to Andy, "Make sure she gets a Kevlar, too."

Even though I've called off the second part of tonight's plan, things can still go wrong.

After we've checked our gear and arms and Casey has put on her bulletproof vest and a coat, I bind her wrists again. I wish I was tying her up for BDSM purposes. Hearing her breath catch, I wonder if she has the same thought. Probably not. I'm sure she hates me right now.

I get into the boat with Casey, Andy, and Tao. My other men have already taken their positions on the island.

"You ever been?" I ask Casey in an attempt to distract her from her fear.

She shakes her head.

"That's the Angel Island Immigration Station," I explain as we pass by a long two-storied building set atop stairs. "It was like Ellis Island for the West Coast. Many immigrants, mostly from China, were detained, interrogated and languished here in the first part of the twentieth century. Today, it's an historical landmark."

"Is that where we're going?" she asks.

"No. We're going to a beach on a different side of the island."

Our boat pulls into a small alcove, hidden from view, though we have equipment that will alert us if the Coast Guard is near. I sweep Casey into my arms and set her on the beach where several of my men and Andrian's men hold either flashlights or assault rifles. She eyes them warily. I want to tell her that it's all going to work out, but I don't know how tonight will play out.

Tao keeps a hand on Casey's arm while Andrian's boat arrives with his men. As he walks past Casey, he snorts. He doesn't like her. Normally Andrian doesn't give a shit about any woman, even the ones he sleeps with, but I know the reason he doesn't like Casey has more to do with me than it does with her.

How did these feelings for Casey sneak up on me? So she was fun to play with. So she's interesting because she's so unlike me: naive, reckless, spoiled even. But she's intelligent, adventurous, daring. She has a fighting spirit. She could be so much more given the right conditions. I remember when I first took Athena off the streets. She was weak and paranoid. The smallest noises made her jump, she barked at everyone, and was afraid to come out of her den. But with time and a better environment, she began to thrive. Now she's strong, confident, and happy to venture afar.

But the fact remains that Casey is the enemy. I need to stay focused on what matters most: getting the SVATR laptop back in my hands.

Half an hour later we hear the speedboats bringing Callaghan and six of his men. The laptop is handcuffed to a redheaded man with a full beard. Casey gasps as she sees her father.

"Did they hurt you, Casey?" he asks her.

She shakes her head. "I'm fine."

Kenton Brady steps forward. "They better not have hurt you."

Andrian snorts.

Brady turns to him. "What the fuck does that mean?"

"Nothing," I intervene. From what I've learned about Brady, he can be temperamental. I do not want two hotheads screwing up the exchange.

"They hurt you, didn't they? Touched you?" Brady asks Casey.

Casey glances at me and insists, "I'm fine."

Brady eyes me with suspicion. Ignoring him, I instruct Callaghan to set the laptop on a table my men had set up in advance. Callaghan nods at the redhead.

The laptop remains tethered to the man while Nikita walks over to check that the laptop is indeed the one we pilfered from SVATR and that it still contains the artificial intelligence software. Everyone remains tensely silent as Nikita clicks away at the keyboard.

"Is good," he finally declares.

"My daughter," Callaghan demands.

"Take the handcuff off the laptop," I reply.

The redhead unlocks the handcuffs. I take Casey from Tao, keeping a hand on her while Callaghan takes her other arm. Andy reaches for the laptop. From the corners of my eyes, I see Brady shift about nervously. Once Andy has the laptop in his possession, I let go of Casey. Callaghan pulls her to him. Seeing Brady gesture to one of his men, I realize something is up. But before I can alert anyone, smoke grenades go off at our feet.

"*Blyad'!*" Andrian swears.

Next comes gunfire. Shit! They're shooting at us. Our men fire back. I try to make my way to where Casey might be, but the smoke is too thick. I can't see shit. I need to get out of this smoke. A hit to my chest causes me to stumble. Luckily the Kevlar saved me from that bullet. Coughing, I manage to stumble out of the smoke and gunfire. Wiping my eyes, I see Brady pulling Casey over to one of the boats. He has the laptop, too.

Relief washes over me when I see that Casey appears to be unharmed. I run over, but Brady turns and fires his gun several times. He misses, but it stops me, giving him time to start the boat and pull away. I hop into one of our boats. Brady fires his gun at me again. I duck. I want nothing more than to pull out my gun and fire back, but I don't want to hit Casey.

Brady's next shot burns hot lead into my arm. The good news is he's out of bullets unless he has a second gun. I hit top speed in the boat and catch up to him through the choppy waters. Brady tries to gun it and lose me by swerving sharply. A wave hits the side of the boat simultaneously, sending Casey tumbling into the water. I'm sure she knows how to swim, but I can't take the chance. The water is freezing, that Kevlar is an extra seven pounds on her, and she still has her hands tied behind her back.

I cut the engine and dive in after Casey. The water is black. The sky is also black thanks to the clouds covering the moon. All I can make out are the city lights in the distance and the lights from the boat. I can't see Casey. Fuck.

"Casey!" I shout as I cast my gaze about, trying to penetrate the darkness.

Fuck. Fuck. Fuck.

"Casey!"

And then I hear my name. It's faint, but loud enough for me to gauge the direction it's coming from. I hear her gasp and make out the water washing over her.

"I've got you," I tell her. "Tread hard for me."

Luckily, I've tied and untied rope so many times, I can do it blindfolded. After undoing her binds, I haul her through the water toward the boat. She grabs the side and pulls herself in while I push her up. Not until we're both in the boat do I realize how much my arm burns and aches from being shot and just how fucking cold the Bay is.

"You all right?" I ask her. "Were you shot?"

While shivering, she shakes her head. I start digging through the boat and manage to find towels stored beneath the seats.

"Get out of your wet clothes," I instruct, helping her with her coat, the Kevlar, and then her sweats before wrapping her in the towels.

After shedding my soaking jacket, I take off my shirt and rip a strip off to tie around my arm. Though I grew up in Heihe, where temperatures can fall below zero in winter, the Bay feels freezing right now.

"My dad," she says.

"You've got to get warmed up."

"I'll be okay."

"Ever heard of hypothermia?"

"If we don't turn around, I'll s-swim back. My dad may be a jerk, but he's still my dad."

I look back to the island but we're not close enough for me to make out the situation. I shake my head. "It's too dangerous."

She throws off the towels. "Fine."

I grab her. "I'll check on your dad for you."

She looks at me with worry. "To help him or hurt him?"

"Help him," I answer truthfully, though I'm not sure whether she'll believe me.

She stares deep into my eyes. "I probably shouldn't trust you, but..."

"You don't have much of a choice."

"Yeah. That."

Just then I hear the rumble of another boat approaching. Seeing only the vehicle's headlights, I grab my 0.45 and get ready to hit the gas.

"Kai!" a familiar voice calls out.

It's Tao. But I keep my firearm raised in case he's not alone. I swing the light in his direction. He's alone.

Seeing me bare-chested and wet, he asks, "Fuck, what happened to you?"

Ignoring his question, I ask him about the situation back on the beach.

"We've got it under control, thanks to our guys on the perimeter," Tao answers as he takes off his coat to hand to me.

I give the coat to Casey.

"What about my dad?" she demands.

Tao looks to me.

"How's Callaghan?" I ask.

"Alive."

"Who else?"

"A Callaghan man, the red-haired guy. Unless Andrian shot him. Andy persuaded him to wait for you before dealing with Callaghan."

"So it's safe to return."

"Yes, but we counted the bodies, and there's a guy missing."

"Brady," I supply. "He's long gone with the laptop."

"Shit."

"We'll hunt him down later."

My body has started to shake, but I tell Tao to head back to the beach. I follow behind in my boat. As we near the island, I see Andrian pacing back and forth. Callaghan is on the ground, possibly wounded, propped up on one elbow. The redhead lies lifeless on the beach along with the other men Callaghan had brought with him.

After beaching the boat, I hand the gun to Casey. "Take this as a precaution. At the first sign of danger, you take the boat and get out of here. Got it?"

She nods.

To Tao, I say, "Stay with her and make sure nothing happens to her."

Seeing me as I hop out of the boat, Andrian strides over. "You get the laptop?"

"No," I answer.

He kicks the sand. "*Blyad'!*"

Andy takes off his coat and hands it to me. I notice his hand is wrapped and bloody.

"Jay didn't make it," Andy reports to me. "And Lev is critical. Our doctor is on his way."

Andrian, still cursing, returns to Callaghan and raises his gun, saying, "Time to die, *ublyudok*."

"It wasn't my idea!" Callaghan objects.

"It doesn't matter! I'm going to shoot all seven rounds into you and watch you bleed to death."

Seeing that Andrian's hand is shaking with rage, I intervene. "We should focus our attention on getting Kenton Brady before he hops a plane to who knows where."

"But first we take care of Callaghan. We agreed he has to pay a price."

"I think he's learned his lesson."

Andrea looks at me like I'm crazy. "What are you talking about? Is it because of that Irish slut? You going soft on me, Kai?"

"I want to go after Kenton Brady. Callaghan might be useful for that."

"Fuck that. Callaghan deserves to die and you know it. Don't let a little piece of pussy mess with your mind."

At that, Andrian turns back around to face Callaghan and shoots him in the thigh. Callaghan emits a roar of pain.

"Enough!" I say.

But another shot cracks the air. I feel the blood drain from me. My first thought, because the shot didn't come from Andrian, was that Casey was in danger. But when I look her way, I see her standing in the boat, holding the type of gun as if she's used one all her life. I look back at Andrian, who has crumpled to his knees. He falls flat on his face next, a gaping hole in his skull.

Andrian's men immediately raise their firearms.

"*Ostanovit'!*" I command in Russian as I place myself between Andrian's men and Casey.

Glancing down at Andrian's prone body, I know there's no way he's surviving a clean shot to the head. Casey has miraculous aim.

My men have also raised their guns, but they're not entirely convinced where to aim. Casey would be the natural target except Tao is acting as her human shield.

This is a fucking mess.

Once Lukashenko, Andrian's superior, learns of Andrian's death, the Bratva is going to go after Casey. So I can't let Lukashenko know. I've got to get rid of the witnesses.

My gaze meets Andy's. I expect him to know what I'm thinking.

"Matters of the heart?" he replies in our native language.

I snort. It's too crazy for me to contemplate at the moment. But Andy's rarely wrong.

"Andrian was a brother to me," I say solemnly in Russian to his men. The only emotion I truly have the wherewithal to acknowledge over the death of my lifelong friend is shock. I don't have the time and capacity to do anything more with Casey's life in danger. "Without him, I probably wouldn't be standing here today. Allow me to take care of this."

I take an AR from Antonne and walk toward Casey. I see her brow furrow in confusion as she moves to hide fully behind Tao, who doesn't know if he should move out of the way or not.

"Step aside," I say in Russian, even though Tao doesn't speak the language.

From the corners of my eyes, I see that Andrian's men have lowered their guard. Spinning around, I empty the whole magazine. It takes less than a minute to down all of them. Andy walks over to inspect the carnage. Seeing one still moving, he fires his pistol into the guy's head.

Handing Antonne back his AR, I walk over to Callaghan, who's curled in a fetal position with his arms over his head.

Crouching down, I tell him, "You owe me big, Liam."

"I swear it wasn't my idea to double cross you!" he says. "I wouldn't risk my daughter's life like that."

"Then why did you bring Brady in the first place?"

"He said he cared about Casey and wanted to help make sure she was okay."

"Which is why he left her in the Bay to drown."

Callaghan looks over at Casey, still half dressed, her hair frozen wet. He lowers his gaze.

"As the head of your organization, the buck stops with you," I continue. "And here's what's going to happen next: first, you're going to help me get the SVATR laptop back from Brady. Then you and your son are going to go back to the East Coast, and you're never going to set foot in California again. Last but not least, you owe me your life. Trust me when I say I very much want to kill you right now. But I'm going to let you live. In your place, I'm going to take hers."

He looks up at me in alarm. "What?"

"Casey's not yours anymore. She's mine. Just remember that if you even think about failing one of my directives."

Standing up, I head over to the boat to see if Casey's okay. But between the cold and the loss of blood from getting shot, I feel faint. I stumble and fall to the sand. The last thing I see before passing out is Casey running toward me.

Chapter Thirty

Casey

A cloud had passed in front of the moon, so I couldn't make out the expression on Kai's face as he walked toward me, holding some kind of semiautomatic rifle. For a split second, I thought I was as good as dead, whatever desire he had had to save me, was wiped out when his friend Andrian hit the beach with a bullet in his head. A bullet I had put there. I'm not even sure if I had intended to kill him. All I know is I wanted to stop him from hurting my dad.

But then the cloud moved, and my gaze met Kai's. He wasn't going to kill me. I didn't expect him to turn around and use the gun on Andrian's men, however. The man I later learned was named Tao remained standing in front of me, shielding me from seeing most of it, though I did glimpse blood spraying through the air. What I mainly saw afterwards was Kai slumping to the ground. I couldn't help him, however, because I stumbled myself. It felt hard to think straight, and my body was still shivering.

I don't remember much of what happened after that. The coat and towels wrapping me were stripped away. A hard and naked body - I think Tao's - embraced me. Eventually, I was transferred to a different boat, one with heating. I heard the man who must be Kai's second in command issue orders for the bodies on the beach. I lost all consciousness after that.

"I feel fine," I protest from my hospital bed to a man named Andy.

"I told you that Kai is doing well," he replies. "I'm not lying."

"I just want to see for myself."

"You can get out a bed when the doctor clears you."

I contemplate defying Andy, but even though he has a gentler expression than Kai, he doesn't look like he'll accept any more crap than his boss would. He also seems to know better than to trust me because he takes a seat opposite my bed, crossing one leg over the other.

"Will the doctor be here soon?" I ask.

"Yes. She should be here any minute, along with your father."

I sit up straighter. "How is he?"

"The surgery to extract the bullet from his leg was successful."

Andy got up at a knock on the door. He opened it to let in my dad, who hobbled in on crutches.

"I'll be outside if you need me," Andy tells me.

The door closes behind him. An awkward silence between me and my father follow. I'm relieved that he's okay, but I'm also pissed as hell at him.

"Where'd you learn to shoot like that?" my father asks.

"Luck of the Irish," I reply.

He nods. "You probably saved my life."

"Probably?! You don't know that Andrian guy well."

"And you do?"

"Thanks to you, I know more about him than I ever wanted to. How did you end on the bad side of a Triad *and* Bratva?"

"I couldn't pass up the tip we had. I came out to Frisco to carve out my own. I guess I underestimated the *Jing San*."

"If it wasn't for Kai...People here don't use the word 'Frisco,' by the way."

My father narrows his eyes at me. "What's the deal between you and Kai anyway? How long have you guys been seeing each other?"

"Not long. I didn't know he was Triad."

Not that that would have necessarily stopped me. I've never been more attracted to a man before.

"And he's why you weren't interested in Kenton?"

"I'll never be interested in Kenton. He's not my type."

"But a Triad boss is?"

"You and I would both be dead if it weren't for him. We owe him. He's risking war with the gang of his childhood friend for us."

"You mean for *you*."

I consider how Kai could have gone after Kenton and the laptop. Instead, he dove into the water to save me.

"But how long will his interest in you last?" my father continues. "Seems like he's reckless and unpredictable, taking on the Bratva."

"You can keep underestimating Kai, but I don't think it's smart to do so."

"And I wouldn't trust a Triad guy if I were you."

"Like you trusted Kenton?" I shoot back.

My father shifts uncomfortably. "Well, looks like there won't be a merger between the Bradys and Callaghans. We could have done something out here in California."

"Not likely. You got burned on someone else's turf. You're better off in Boston."

"Guess I have no choice now, but what's going to happen to you?"

"I want to stay in California."

"What about Notre Dame?"

"I'm done. If I want to go to college, I'll try UC Merced."

My father doesn't look happy, but I'm no longer the little girl trying to appease her father for a grain of affection. But I am grateful that he made an attempt to give up the laptop for me, even though it's the least a loving father could have done.

"Thanks for doing the exchange," I say.

My father releases a breath and mumbles, "I...I'm sorry about what happened."

I stare at him. My father has *never* apologized to me before.

The door opens. Andy and a doctor walk in.

"Hi, I'm Doctor Chen," the woman says. "I'm just going to check your vitals."

Andy says to my father, "Two of my guys will take you home now. Your flight back to Boston is booked for tomorrow."

My father looks at me. I don't think the two of us will ever have a close and loving relationship, but I'm okay with that. He's going to let me live my own life—he has no choice, really—and that's all I want for now.

"I'd take a break from the Mob if I were you," I say. "Maybe a permanent break."

He nods. "Not bad advice. Bye, Casey."

After my father leaves, the doctor examines me and clears me. I hop out of bed immediately, then look down at my hospital gown. I wish I had something nicer on, but I just want to see Kai as soon as possible.

Andy leads me to Kai's room down the hall. Turns out we're not actually at any legitimate hospital but a facility run by the *Jing San*.

Inside Kai's room stands Tao and another guy. Tao and I exchange glances. I blush. I'm pretty sure we were naked together on the boat while he was trying to warm up my body with his. Hell, he was probably one of the guys in the gangbang.

Pushing away my initial embarrassment, I grin at him. "Hey, Tao. Thanks for saving me from hypothermia."

He grins back. "Anytime."

"Like hell he will," says Kai as he steps forward.

I drink in the sight of Kai, looking as hot as ever. He has on a loose tank, bandages around his arm, and sweatpants. I wonder if he's commando under those pants.

Kai nods at the door to his men. They file out of the room, leaving the two of us alone.

Suddenly, I feel shy. I don't think I've ever felt shy in front of Kai before.

I look at his arm. "How badly did you get shot?"

"I'm fine."

He got shot for me. Or maybe for that laptop. But given that he opted to save me instead of going after Kenton, I'm guessing not so much the laptop.

"So what happens now?" I ask.

He pulls me into him. Heat flares through me as soon as I hit his body.

He cups the back of my head. "You mean now that you belong to me?"

My breath catches. I desperately want him to kiss me, but he only gazes at my lips.

"How come you get real clothes and I'm in this?" I ask with pretend anger.

He raises a brow. "It's more than you've had on most of our time together."

My face grows hot. "Yeah, well, I'm ready to put on some nice clothes and have a super fancy meal to celebrate being alive."

His hand moves from the back of my head to my jaw. "Still a princess."

I suppress a smile. "You wanna do something about it?"

He pins me with his stare. "You bet I do."

I look about the uninspiring room with its hospital bed, monitors, and IVs. "Not here?"

"I think we pay another visit to The Lotus."

I perk up. "Yes! But you know...maybe we could mess around a little here first."

He shakes his head with a bemused grin. "You have a one-track mind, Casey Callaghan."

Lowering his head, he claims my mouth. This kiss feels every bit as amazing as the prospect of spending hours submitting to his skills as a Dom. I press my lips hard against his, feeling victorious because it turns out the 'princess' is pretty damn good at ensnaring dragons.

~*~

Looking for a little more naughty steam? As a thank-you for your purchase of *Captured Mafia Princess*, you can get a bonus epilogue by clicking here or at https://www.darksteamybooks.com/capt ured-mafia-princess-bonus. Find out what Kai has in store for Casey when they return to The Lotus for some BDSM fun.

Made in the USA
Coppell, TX
31 May 2024

32967804R00174